STOWAWAY

STOWAWAY

STOWAWAY

PAM WITHERS

DUNDURN
TORONTO

Cover image: FOG: Shutterstock.com/leolintang BOAT: shutterstock.com/Girts Pavlins
Printer: Webcom

Library and Archives Canada Cataloguing in Publication

Withers, Pam, author

    Stowaway / Pam Withers.
Issued in print and electronic formats.
ISBN 978-1-4597-4191-1 (softcover).--ISBN 978-1-4597-4192-8 (PDF).--
ISBN 978-1-4597-4193-5 (EPUB)

    I. Title.

PS8595.I8453S76 2018   jC813'.6   C2017-907455-5

                                            C2017-907456-3

1 2 3 4 5   22 21 20 19 18

We acknowledge the support of the **Canada Council for the Arts**, which last year invested $153 million to bring the arts to Canadians throughout the country, and the **Ontario Arts Council** for our publishing program. We also acknowledge the financial support of the **Government of Ontario**, through the **Ontario Book Publishing Tax Credit** and the **Ontario Media Development Corporation**, and the **Government of Canada**.

Nous remercions le Conseil des arts du Canada de son soutien. L'an dernier, le Conseil a investi 153 millions de dollars pour mettre de l'art dans la vie des **Canadiennes et des Canadiens** de tout le pays.

Care has been taken to trace the ownership of copyright material used in this book. The author and the publisher welcome any information enabling them to rectify any references or credits in subsequent editions.

— *J. Kirk Howard, President*

The publisher is not responsible for websites or their content unless they are owned by the publisher.

Printed and bound in Canada.

VISIT US AT

dundurn.com | @dundurnpress | dundurnpress | dundurnpress

Dundurn
3 Church Street, Suite 500
Toronto, Ontario, Canada
M5E 1M2

PROLOGUE

Guatemala City, Guatemala

ARTURO

Crack! Crack!

The sound of gunshots rips my eyes open and sends rats scurrying across the abandoned warehouse.

"Try in there!" Men's shouts make me spring up from the dirt-coated concrete floor, where the kids and I have been dozing in a corner.

Fifteen pairs of sleep-deprived eyes widen and turn to me in the near-total darkness. Small, grimy hands reach out to grip my arm, but no one makes a sound. Not so much as a whimper. I have trained them well.

"Follow me!" I whisper. I grab my backpack and roll through the hole in the crumbling brick wall beside us. The night's fresh, salty air fills my lungs as I get to my feet and head for the bay. I twist around once, just in time to see the last child crawl through the gap seconds before the watchmen's powerful flashlights shine there. In the pre-dawn stillness, the soft pounding of the youngsters' feet behind me gives wind to my own.

Not a night passes that I don't have a backup plan. It is why my contingent of street kids and I are still alive. Tonight, I'm aiming for the empty Dumpster beside the shipyard, no more than a two-minute sprint away.

But I worry about them all fitting inside. The size of my group has become unwieldy.

"Too many of us," pants Freddy, my second-in-command, not for the first time.

At eleven, he's the oldest and most street-savvy of them all — ready, we've agreed, to take command of his own pack soon. My group is dangerously large because, unlike other teen leaders, I don't beat my charges. And when bruised, battered, homeless boys show up after defecting from other clans, I don't have the heart to turn away these mirror images of my six-year-old self.

"Take half the boys tomorrow," I tell Freddy as we reach the Dumpster. "Or all if I get whacked."

His lips curl into a grim smile.

The slight squeak as I lift the Dumpster lid is drowned out by our pursuers' continued shouts. I cup my hands to hoist the youngest boy up by his foot, like I once saw a rich man lifting his child onto a saddled pony. With the older boys helping, they're soon all up and over. Freddy throws himself on top of the squirming pile, shushing them as I lower the lid.

"Get him!" a guard shouts, and I know it is time to dart away, to direct the armed posse elsewhere, like a mother bird with a faked limp.

Crack! Crack! Heart flipping and ears ringing with the noise of bullets whizzing over my head, I leap onto the deck of a docked yacht and scurry to the far side. They won't risk damaging it by shooting at me now.

I grab a life ring and toss it, hoping the splash will make the men think I have leapt into the bay. But when I lift my head, I'm blinded by lights flaring inside the yacht. *Shit.*

A shadow stomping up the companionway turns into a large man who grabs me by an ear. The searing pain drops me to my knees. He's going to tear it right off.

"That's him!" a voice on shore behind a spotlight shouts as my captor pulls me into view.

"The rest are in the Dumpster!" comes a victorious cry farther back. "Fish in a barrel, boys!"

Heart-piercing screams make me sink the rest of the way to the deck. As I lie limp and numb, the faces of the kids I have been protecting for months swim before me.

"Don't know who you're chasing." The big man's deep voice addresses the guard on shore. "But this here boy is with me. My first mate. Nothing to do with whoever you just got. But good on you for keeping the street-kid population down. Have a nice evening."

CHAPTER ONE

Horton Island, British Columbia, Canada
Three Years Later

OWEN

I sit on our dock, the tips of my shoes in the frigid May water, forty-nine kinds of bored. Nothing ever happens around here. It's Dullsville without the ville.

I've devised a punishment for parents who move to an island so small that it doesn't even have a school. For starters, they should be wrapped in seaweed and left at low tide for jellyfish to sting and seagulls to guano-bomb.

There's no one close to my age on this entire three-mile-long, sea-locked lump of dirt and trees. I have to catch a water taxi (named *The Scholarship*, ha ha) to the nearest island with a high school, where I get treated like a redneck just 'cause the kids on that island are thirty-nine kinds of bored.

Since today is Saturday and the local Coast Guard officer is away, I leap up and move along the dock, scanning the dozen boats in our marina for one to joyride later this afternoon. Then I can cruise around, swipe cans of beer from locked-up summer cabins, and shoot fish with my air gun. Or step into Charlie Aitkens's bull pasture and play chicken with Ruffian, his two-thousand-pound beast with a bony head and a neck thick like a mobster's.

One day I'm going to leave this rain-soaked smidgen of sod and really see the world. Have adventures. Cruise out of one of the Coast Guard academies with honours. Save dinghies in distress. Till then, all I can do to keep myself from going brain-dead is train my binoculars on passing ships and dream I'm escaping on them. Or play ring toss with life ring buoys, which I'm actually pretty good at.

Just as I'm selecting a twenty-five-foot cabin cruiser on our dock as my getaway vehicle, my mother's bullhorn voice sounds from above.

"Owen! Ohhhhh-wen!" Her call is all but drowned out by the noise she's making clanging the ship's bell fastened to our house on the cliff above. "Luuuunch!"

My runners squeak to a halt on a slimy board. Perfect. After lunch she and Dad have to catch a ferry to a plane. Which means I've got a Get Out of Jail Free card.

"Coming, Mom!"

I sprint along the dock and count all 120 steps up to our house for the 1,120th time, not pausing on any of them. I savour the burning in my calves 'cause I'm all about fitness, as all future Coast Guard officers should be.

"So, Owen," my dad says, tugging on his beard as he clicks his suitcase shut, "you've read the list of stuff you need to do while we're away?"

"Replace those two rotting steps, shovel up the otter poop, swab the slime off the dock, change the oil on the two ketches, and fuel up any customers who stop in."

My parents own Steward Marina. It's one of only four fine business establishments on this West Coast islet, along with the hardware store, bakery, and general store. My current occupation is marina maintenance slave and sometime spy, and my goal is to be captain of a very large ship elsewhere. At the very least, I aspire to escape this worthless wart of woodland and become a wayward wanderer. Soon.

"That's my boy," Dad says, like I'm ten instead of sixteen. Usually I'm mistaken for even older than I am, given my height and stylin' soul patch. But parents have a way of shrinking you.

Dad pushes the day's newspaper at me. "Another ghost ship story. A condemned cattle freighter they bought from a scrapyard." He shakes his head and frowns. "What's this world coming to?"

"In Europe?" I ask as I take the paper from him and scan the story. Illegal immigrants from the Middle East and Africa have been washing up on Europe's shores for a while, dead or alive depending on their ships, the weather that week, and local rescue efforts. But the ghost ship stories are the most haunting: immigrants paying for a berth on a boat that their handlers abandon mid-channel.

"Yeah, they locked up the passengers in the freighter's animal pens, jammed the controls, and took off in motorized lifeboats. So there was no pilot aboard as it tore across the Mediterranean at nine knots. Would've shipwrecked if the Coast Guard hadn't eventually managed to board and evacuate it."

"Twisted," I say. "And it must've been a complicated job for the rescuers."

"Yeah," Dad says grimly. "Be glad we live in Canada."

"Boats of illegals come to Canada too, sometimes."

"Not often, and we've never had a ghost ship incident," Dad replies.

"Stop being all doom and gloom, you two," Mom speaks up. "So, Owen, chores, as we were discussing."

"Chores," Dad echoes as he snatches the paper back with a smirk.

"Yes, ma'am." I sit up straight.

"Water the houseplants and don't have any wild parties." She sets plates and a carafe of hot coffee on the table.

"Aw, but I've invited all my friends over to drink and do drugs." If I had any friends on the island, that would worry her. It pains me that she knows it's not even a possibility. They kind of made sure of that by moving here three years ago. Snatched me away from friends they didn't like.

"You're certain you'll be okay for an entire week?" she asks, leaning over to kiss my head as I duck. "We've never left you this long before. I feel kind of bad going with your dad and leaving you all on your own. Mrs. Aitkens isn't far if you need anything, and I've frozen two casseroles —"

"Mom, I'm fine. Enjoy the marina managers' conference and bring me back some pictures of Miami."

"You're sure?" She glances at her suitcase by the door like she's ready to unpack it and stay.

I lift a sandwich from the platter and pour coffee into my mug. "You remembered cream and sugar! You're the best!"

I'm laying it on so they'll chill, but the truth is, I really do have a thing for coffee with cream and sugar.

"One more thing, Owen," Dad says as he helps himself to a sandwich.

"Yeah?"

"Weather forecast is a big storm tomorrow. So take extra care —"

"Securing all the boats for the clients who park 'em with us. Especially the boats I like," I tease.

He tries to smile. So does Mom. But the word *storm* always conjures up unwelcome memories. It prompts all three of us to look out to the bay at the same time. We see patches of darkness in the shifting water. Shadows whose shapes differ for each of us. Just as quickly, we turn our gazes elsewhere — anywhere but in one another's eyes.

We came all the way across the country to escape it. But the memory is still with us.

• • •

ARTURO

The stray slap of a wave against the yacht's hull wakes me with a start. I twist around fast in the captain's seat, bracing for the bite of Captain Carlos Maldave's lashing belt, and I let my breath out only when I see my boss asleep, his drooping belly draped over the cushions of the two-seat unit behind the captain's seat.

I sit up straighter and look ahead, stroking my cricked neck. Falling asleep on watch is the most serious offence on board, and I'm furious with myself. Rubbing my eyes and peering east, I watch a pool of blood-red seep across the bottom of the indigo sky until dawn converts it to pink and spews it over the surface of the Pacific Ocean.

"Red sky at night, sailor's delight. Red sky at morning, sailor's warning." Captain's deep, gruff voice instantly jerks my body to attention. "What does it mean, Arturo?" he continues in Spanish.

I know it is a challenge; a test I had better pass. And I will. "Red sky at morning means a low-pressure system moving east, Captain," I reply in Spanish. "It means a storm is on the way." I stop myself from adding, "Right?" because Captain hates uncertainty.

"Smart kid for a shoeshine boy," Captain responds with a chuckle.

I wince at the reference to my former job and recall the night he saved my life.

After the guards had left us, the captain leaned down and helped me to my feet. "My first mate just ran off, so I'm offering you the job."

I knew it was not a choice; clearly he would turn me in if I turned him down. But the gentle touch of his hand on my shoulder fooled me. I interpreted it as a trace of kindness. I believed he understood the pain flooding my chest and the crushing guilt of losing the pack of street kids I had trained and protected with everything I had.

It was barely a tap, and almost never since repeated. But the touch felt warm, a balm of relief applied to my shattered self, and it ignited in me a desperate need for someone who cared, someone who might take care of me — a father, like in the movies.

"When opportunity presents itself, take it," he continued.

"Yes," I agreed.

And look at what I've been able to do since then, thanks to the captain: travel the West Coast from Central America to Canada and back several times, learn to manage the customers, and best of all, get handy at running *Archimedes*, the forty-five-foot luxury yacht ploughing north under our direction right now.

"You learn fast," he said once. Translation: I have learned to anticipate his orders and act before getting belted more often than not. My ready-for-anything survival instincts continue to serve me well.

"Keep it up and I'll give you a raise," Captain mumbles now with a half yawn as he sits up and scratches his barrel chest through his worn undershirt.

I brighten a little. A raise. It's a promise that keeps me going, allows me sometimes to imagine a future beyond Captain and *Archimedes*. I am building a stash of cash in a tin can hidden under a floorboard in the broom closet for the day I decide to escape — or the day Captain turns on me. Whichever comes first.

With that money and the English I'm working hard to pick up, sometimes I dare to dream. I imagine myself running a little breakfast cafe in Guatemala City, serving both locals and tourists. I imagine getting hired for my cooking skills and the fact that I can get by in English. I'll have to speak slowly, of course, because of my accent, so I've been told. I'm working on that.

Born in Los Angeles to San Salvadorian parents, Captain is fluent in Spanish, yet also speaks English without an accent, which comes in handy in his profession. And sometimes he or a sympathetic client gives me English lessons.

"How old are you now, anyway?" Captain asks, breaking into my thoughts.

"Sixteen, Captain." Truth is, I am not sure exactly how old I am, having been on my own for so long. But I overheard some of the private-school boys who boarded *Archimedes* two weeks ago telling Captain they were sixteen, and they seemed the same age as me.

Captain and the customers think I don't understand much English, but over the years working on the yacht, I've picked up way more than they think, and I understand it better than I speak it.

"Coffee, Captain? Breakfast?"

"*Pronto*, boy."

I exit the captain's seat and take the companionway steps down to the galley kitchen. I lift the black metal frying pan from its rack, drop in the refried beans, cheese, and bananas, and start the coffee maker. Then I bend down to breathe in the magical aroma of the fresh grounds. Same breakfast every day. But I am lucky he lets me eat any leftovers. Way better than having to search dumpsters for half-rotten food and getting shot at for it.

"Burn the beans again today, and I'll bust your jaw," the captain shouts from the pilothouse.

Hopefully a joke. With one eye on the breakfast in progress, I look through the window into the pilothouse, where the captain is studying his navigational aids. There, too, I know way more than I let on.

"Are we in Canada yet?" I dare to ask.

Steely eyes in an unshaven face turn on me, and there's silence but for the creaking of the boat. At last my boss utters one word: "Tonight."

CHAPTER TWO

OWEN

"Warning shot across the bow," Coast Guard Officer Allen Olsen advises me. "They're not answering Channel 16."

Channel 16, of course, is the 24-7 Coast Guard channel that all boats should listen to in case they need to respond to a mayday call: an emergency.

"They've cut power, sir," I confirm, my pulse pounding in my ears mosh-pit hard and my hands sweatier than my armpits.

"Okay, alert crew to board to starboard. Steady as she goes. Now hard to port and come alongside."

"Are our guys wearing bulletproof vests?" I ask my mentor as I grip the throttle quadrant of our twenty-nine-foot patrol cutter.

"No."

"It's an old wooden Packer. Has seen better days. Could be hiding up to forty illegals," I estimate.

"Concentrate on controls, Owen. Steady. Okay, ease in gently." He grabs the bullhorn and directs it at the vessel, now just yards away. "We repeat. Canadian Coast Guard orders you to stand down for boarding."

Bzzzt!

"Hey!" I shout, pouting. "Game can't be over yet. It was just getting good!"

Officer Olsen grins, pushes the off button on his laptop-sized console, and rests a hand on my shoulder. Then he says what he always says whenever we run through one of his simulator-training exercises in Horton Island's tiny Coast Guard station office. "Not a game, Owen, and if my supervisor ever gets word I let an underage non-cadet do simulation modules, he'll keelhaul me."

"No one will hear it from me," I promise. Lifting my head, I spot a *WANTED* printout on the bulletin board featuring a police sketch of a bearded man. "Hey, a new Coast Guard alert. What's it about?"

"There have been two on-water robberies in this region," he replies, following my eyes to the board.

"Pirates? Seriously?" Not unheard of, but as rare as the Loch Ness monster in this part of the world.

"A group of hoodlums in a rigid-hulled inflatable who think they can get away with it. Led by a Caucasian man with a grey beard. We're on it; we'll catch them."

"Of course you will. I'll keep an eye out."

"You do that, Owen."

"Any tips from the exercise we just did?" Usually he gives me advice after one of our simulator sessions.

He sits back and strokes his chin for a moment, all too serious looking. "Why are you so set on joining the Coast Guard, Owen?"

I look up in surprise. He has never asked that before. "So I can save people," I answer in a measured tone.

He nods, keeps nodding, making me nervous with his silence. "You know it won't change what happened back in Ontario."

I leap up, flushed. "It doesn't have anything to do with that!"

He stands slowly and faces me as if to create a force field that will quiet me down and make me sit again.

"Tips?" he echoes, and looks me straight in the eye. "Don't ever do anything illegal. The Coast Guard won't hire someone with a criminal conviction."

"Of course," I say in a choked voice. There's no way he could know the truth of what happened in Ontario.

I glance out the office's window. "Whoa! Look, Officer Olsen!"

A glut of heavy clouds is taking over the sky like an oil spill. Good thing my parents' plane got out yesterday.

"That storm's finally arriving. Looks like it's going to let loose any minute. Want me to drive you home?"

I shake my head. "No thanks. Biking's good. I appreciate the practice, Officer Olsen. Maybe see you tomorrow."

"Not tomorrow, Owen. I'm off-island. But call me if you need anything, anytime."

As I bike home, the weather spills like a collapsing tarp roof. Given that the Coast Guard office and our marina are at opposite ends of Horton Island, I'm doomed to get 150 percent soaked as I sprint along the curvy blacktopped road between giant swaying Douglas firs and cedars.

Truth is, I love approaching storms. It's fun watching them hit the island like a giant boxing glove. Window-panes rattle and tin roofs do heavy-metal riffs. Small branches come flying off of trees. Eagles cling to tree-tops by their claws, *pip-pip-pip*-ing as they sway in the gusts. Animals go into hiding and people tuck up into their cabins. And it goes dark so fast.

As I step onto the deck of our house, I hear the jingling of loose rigging in the bay below. The boats shift like restless horses in a corral. I slip inside and by the time I've made myself a cup of coffee, all hell has broken loose. The boats in the marina, large and small, go into gang warfare: elbowing, jostling, trying to punch one another as the swells beneath them get violent.

I've only just shed my dripping bike jacket when a growl of thunder shakes the entire island, and a jagged bolt of lightning highlights the dark ocean like a camera flash. As I light the kindling in the fireplace, howling winds suck the flames halfway up the chimney. And then, just like that, the lights in the house flicker and go out.

Cool. It's going to be a candlelit dinner for one: hot dogs cooked campfire-style in the fireplace. So much for playing chess with one of my internet buddies. Not worth trudging down to the dock to fetch the backup generator for just an hour online.

After fumbling for the matches and our cookie tin full of stubby candles, I look out at the water and wonder if I've secured the marina's boats well enough. That's when a shadow moves silently into the bay. Like a phantom ship, it shudders and pounds in the whipped-up waves, yet steers smoothly to the dock as if it's on an underwater cable.

A slight, barefoot figure leaps from the bow with a thick coil of rope and lashes the craft tightly to the mooring cleats of an empty berth. In the last moments of dusk, the silhouettes of the boat and boy merge with the black of the water and sky, and I know I've entirely imagined the vessel's arrival. *It's not him. Ontario is too far away. Stop fantasizing every time there's a storm. Anyway, there's nothing to fear.*

> Section 6.1c, Moorage Law Covenants: You must provide without compensation temporary accommodation to any vessel that is disabled or that seeks shelter in weather conditions that would render it unseaworthy.

Why did that just pop into my mind?

• • •

I've awakened to a tapping on my bedroom window. Battering swaths of rain, I tell myself. The fire has burned to glowing coals, the candlewicks have punched out early, and my hot dog–stomach ache makes me groan.

Tap, tap, tap. No sane woodpecker would be doing his thing at this time of night, especially not *this* night. I sit up and fold back a flap of the curtain over the window above my bed. A pair of eyes, white with small black pupils, stares back.

"What the —" I release the curtain and dive under my quilt. *A nightmare. You're making things up. Not really awake.*

Tap, tap. "Hello?"

I rise, pull on my frayed red terrycloth bathrobe, grab my headlamp, and unlock the front door. It nearly brains me as it flies back with the force of the wind, and the soaking I take from the rain is like a bucket of water being tossed in my face.

"Hello?" I direct my slightly trembling voice into the darkness.

He appears in front of me: a short, skinny Latino dude in grubby jeans, an oil-stained hoodie, and over-sized white boating shoes that seem to glow in the dark. He wears a headlamp with a pathetically weak beam.

"Sorry, sorry. But please to turn power on at dock? For charging. Our batteries too much low."

The accent is Hispanic, and for a split second he looks almost as nervous as me. Then he's trying to peer past me into our house.

When I don't answer right away, he points toward the marina without taking those bug-eyes off me. "Storm."

"Storm?" I mock-echo. "Oh, and I was just head-ing out for a picnic! You do know it's the middle of the night? Is this an emergency?"

24

Hesitation. Then, "*No emergencia.*"

"Okay, then try me in the morning. Maybe we'll have power by then. The storm took it out."

I start to close the door when he catches it with a bicep that bulges in a way you'd swear such a scrawny guy couldn't manage.

"You alone?"

"Actually, my wife and five children are all here, but sleeping," I say, narrowing my eyes at him while calculating how fast I can scoop up my cellphone from the coffee table and hit Officer Olsen's number.

A flash of surprise, then mistrust, crosses his face. It occurs to me that his English isn't up to catching all I've said.

"No power?" he asks, like he has only just noticed our house is dungeon-dark.

"No power. Storm," I say. "Maybe in the morning."

"Morning," he says dubiously. "But we are gone in morning."

"Not if you have a battery too much low."

His frown indicates he has processed that. "Need diesel and water, too." He mimes drinking so that I know what kind of water.

I sigh. Okay, I'm awake now, and bigger than him, so whatever. Obviously the power cut took out the water pump at the dock. I gesture him in and lead him with my headlamp to our kitchen. Water splashes on my hands as I fill up a two-gallon plastic jug. His eyes travel to the platter of leftover hot dogs I never put away, so I hand him the dish along with a glass of water. A couple of dogs and the water both go down like he's some kind of stranded shipwreck victim.

"I'd offer you coffee, my favourite drink, except I can't heat any up."

"Is okay." He chugs the water down pretty fast, then finds his way to the bathroom and back slowly, sticking his nose and headlamp into my parents' room and then my bedroom for a moment. Snoopy sort.

"Owen," I say, pointing to myself.

"Arturo," he replies.

• • •

ARTURO

This tall guy, Owen, is clearly alone, I'm thinking to myself in Spanish. (I've tried, but I'm not good enough to think in English yet.) And even if he is a little annoyed about being woken up, he is starved for someone to talk to. Maybe the storm has rattled him. Looks like he has no brothers or sisters — not uncommon with gringo families, I've noticed.

"Parents?" I ask.

"Away for a week," the boy answers with a sort of conspiratorial grin. "Freedom! Tomorrow I'm going to head out on one of the boats down there and explore around, camp on islands, fish and stuff."

The gringo boy talks too fast, but I get some of it. "All boats yours?" I question, trying not to sound shocked.

Owen wiggles his eyebrows, which seems such a strange thing to do that I do it back to him, which makes the island boy laugh.

"My parents own the marina. I have keys to some of the boats. And I know how to hot-wire the rest. Not that I would." He says it so proudly that I know to grin at him the same way that I and the other shoeshine boys would after agreeing to get some tourist to pay us triple the going rate.

"I have to make my own fun," Owen continues. "This is the most boring island in the universe!"

Boring island? I let myself dream for a microsecond of having parents and a big house like this on a beautiful island. And keys to a bunch of boats in a marina.

"No friends?" I press, since Owen seems naive enough to answer anything I ask. The new, more sober expression on the tall boy's face notifies me that I have stumbled onto something.

"No one my age. Nothing to do. Except hang out with the Coast Guard officer, who's off-island at the moment, or help fix and service boats with my dad."

"You fix boats?"

"I can fix almost any kind of boat." The gringo boy pushes the plate of cold hot dogs back at me, so I help myself as slowly and politely as I can manage.

"If you're around for a day, I could show you the island, eh? There's a store where you can get food and supplies, even ice cream. Good places to fish, if you like fishing. I caught a twelve-pound salmon last week. And there's a lighthouse and this farm with a bull you wouldn't believe the size of, and —"

He stops like he is embarrassed to have gushed all that so quickly. "How about you, Arturo? Where are you from? Where are you going? What kind of boat are you on? How many people on it? Bet it was exciting out there when the storm hit!"

Questions. Dangerous questions. I look down at the jug of water, stand, and move toward the door.

"We talk in morning," I say firmly. "Maybe I go to store with you then. Thanks for food. And sorry, sorry for I wake you up."

"Oh, no problem," Owen says, leaping up. "Yeah, I'll be down to fuel you up and help you get your batteries recharged when it's light. That's *if* they get the power working by morning. Otherwise there's a generator."

As I exit into the downpour with Owen's cellphone in my jeans pocket, I train my headlamp on the slippery steps that lead down the cliff. I feel Owen's eyes at the dark window, watching me disappear. I have lots of information for Captain, who will be pleased. But maybe I will save some of the information for myself.

CHAPTER THREE

OWEN

I toss and turn as the storm's rage continues to clobber the house. At the first streak of light, I sit up and listen hard. The faceless alarm clock plugged in by my bed indicates the power's still off. Rain continues to smear the window as wind wallops the walls. Last night's encounter comes rushing back.

A strange boat has docked in our marina, I reflect with a mix of anxiety and intrigue. Sheltering from the storm, stuck here till they can resupply. With a boy my age who might hang out with me today! Should I inform Officer Olsen? I leap up and move to the coffee table in the living room. But I must've put the cellphone down somewhere else. Anyway, nah.

I try to guess what kind of vessel it is and from where. Mexico or South America, maybe. In which case it'll be big. Maybe a tramp steamer or forty-foot sailboat or even an offshore cruiser. *Well, you da boss of the marina*, I remind myself. And I handled last night well. Didn't I?

Clothes thrown on, a chocolate bar for breakfast down the gullet, I train my binoculars on the dock. And do a low whistle. A handsome white trawler with a raised pilothouse. Forty-plus feet, I'm guessing. Its profile is familiar.

Too strange to be a coincidence.

My feet pad back to my bedroom, where I face the 9x12 framed photo of my older brother on my dresser. "Gregor, a Hans Christian Independence 45 has pulled up to our dock. It's a sign, right? The same type as our favourite boat back in the Toronto marina. Remember how we used to sneak onto it and pretend to take it places?"

Seriously? he says. *It's totally a sign. Go check it out. Get on board and come pick me up, little brother. We'll have an adventure.*

I laugh bitterly and back away from the frame. "Like that's going to happen! I don't even know who's on it or where it's going. Stranger danger, remember? And Mom and Dad would freak."

A week, Owen. You have a week to do anything you want, go wherever it's going. If the people on board seem okay, go for it. Mom and Dad will never even know. Sorry you're stuck here with no friends at all 'cause of me. I say go have some fun for once. It's a freakin' sign, like you say.

I rub my jaw, then place the photo face down, gently. "Mom and Dad say you're a bad influence on me, Gregor. I'm not listening to you."

Because he's upside down, he doesn't reply the way I know he would.

Minutes later, braced against the wind and wearing a hooded rain poncho, I work my way down the steps to the dock and pause to stare at the yacht. I'm pretty keen to get a look-see at the inside of this baby, and also to suss out if this Arturo dude is up for a day on Horton, including maybe some badass fun, storm or no storm.

Rain runs down my poncho and the wind has me walking tilted. I nearly trip on a rotted step before reaching the dock.

"Ahoy!" says a large man on the bow deck. He has tangled black hair under a mariner's rain hat, a tooth missing from his wide smile, a moustache, and an impressive beer gut. "You must be Owen. Good service here for you to show so early, especially in this lousy weather!"

Arturo appears, half skulking behind the big man who, Mexican or whatever he might be, has no trace of an accent.

"Captain Jones," the man introduces himself, extending a hand between boat and dock.

I wince as he all but breaks mine in his crushing grip. "Nice to meet you, Captain. Power is still out, so I have to start the backup generator to fuel you up and get the water pump happening. There's a general store on the island if you need supplies — opens in a few hours — and if you want any kind of tune-up or oil change, I'm your man."

I notice he glances up the cliff behind me as if to make sure I'm on my own. I note the boat's name: *Archimedes*. Name of Merlin the Magician's owl in that book and animated movie about King Arthur. I take a quick look for the identifying numbers I can look up on the internet, but am disappointed to see a wet towel hanging over where they must be.

"Nice boat," I say as the generator starts up and I shove the nozzle into the fuel tank. "Any damage from the storm? Where are you coming from?"

"From Seattle via Victoria. Cleared customs yesterday," he replies as Arturo studies the deck. "Yeah, pretty scary wave action out there. And the weather report says it won't calm till tonight. No damage, luckily. I was relieved to find your little bay. Is the store within walking distance? I'll send my nephew up for supplies."

"It's a twenty-minute bike ride and I have an extra bike. Maybe I can show him around the island till the store opens?"

The captain hesitates as Arturo polishes a cleat, the wedge-shaped block around which lines are secured.

"Sure, why not?" the big guy replies. Arturo's face breaks into a surprised smile.

"Can I check the bilges, bilge pumps, or fuel lines for you?" I ask, looking for an excuse to see below decks.

The request produces a momentary frown on the captain's face.

"Thanks," he replies at length, "but Arturo's a real wizard with all that. The fuelling is the main thing. After you've filled the tank, we've got twenty ten-gallon jerry cans Arturo will line up for you."

Whoa, a full day's worth of emergency fuel, I think. Why would they need all that? But I keep the question to myself. "Hey, Arturo."

"He doesn't speak much English," the captain warns me. Arturo promptly winks at me from an angle his uncle can't see, as if to say, "That's what *he* thinks." I realize Arturo hasn't spoken a word since my arrival, and I almost get the vibe he's scared of the big guy. Hmm, I think. Not a very chummy uncle-nephew combo.

Thirty minutes later, I've completed the refuelling and jerry-can operation, and the captain places several crisp hundred-dollar bills in my palm. Cash, really?

"Well done," he says as a gust of wind almost takes his hat. "You're very helpful, young man. Okay, Arturo has the list and money. Be back by four. We'll be off as soon as we get a weather window. Don't get too soaked. Maybe I'll have some coffee waiting when you get back."

"Love coffee," I say.

"I know," the captain replies, which doesn't seem odd to me at the time.

• • •

ARTURO

My excitement at being trusted to fetch groceries without the captain ("Captain Jones" indeed — ha!) breathing down my neck is cut short when we reach Owen's house and the boy heads straight to his bedroom, bends down, and pulls a gun out from under his bed.

Heart speeding up, I'm about to dive, roll, and slash Owen with the pocket knife I keep handy, when I realize just in time it is a stupid air pistol. A BB gun, a spring-pistol single-shot .177. Kid stuff. What's with this idiot?

"For blowing fish out of the water or doing target practice on squirrels and beer cans," Owen explains.

"Oh," is all I can manage for a moment. Way smaller than the Glock that Captain keeps strapped to his calf day and night, and more or less useless in a fight. Owen must not have any real guns if he acts so proud of this one.

I know all too much about guns and what they can do. Starting with the time I was maybe six ...

• • •

"Stop! Stop!" my mom is screaming from the other room.

Smack. The sound draws me to the open door, where I stare at my towering stepfather, his back to me, his fists pounding her face and body. *Smack. Crack!*

"Please! No!" comes her cry.

I've watched it many times before, but this time a strange electric current enters my small, trembling body and propels me to the kitchen. I shove a chair under the counter with the drawer I know holds his piece. I clamber up and use both hands to pull it out.

The buzz that's controlling me helps me climb down and return to the doorway. I aim the heavy pistol straight at him, dead certain of what I must do.

"Well, lookie at little Arturo," he says, turning. His face is puffy like the bread dough my mom works sometimes, but red, with small mean eyes that sizzle like lit sparklers.

"Arturo!" Mom lets out a scream.

I try to hold as still as a statue in the wind, but there's a howling at the edge of the storm I don't like: it's my giant-sized stepfather chortling and laughing as he lunges. The cold press of the metal is torn from my hand. Then massive fleshy fingers close around my neck and lift me up, up, up.

A door yanks itself open and the stairs to the lower landing appear, tilted and twisting. I go tumbling down them, somersaulting from the top to the faraway bottom. The landing rises to punch the breath out of my chest and turn everything to black. It somehow puts me to sleep.

Click click. A mouse wakes me as it scurries past. I open an eye where I'm curled up, shivering and bruised, on a round rag mat surrounded by muddy-smelling boots.

Achoo! The dust of the mat makes me sneeze.

Slowly, in the morning's first light, I crawl up the stairs to our apartment door, though my knees feel like giant bruises and a fiery pain keeps shooting down my neck. I stand tall to reach the doorknob. It won't turn. I slump down and wait.

When it bursts open, he appears, unshaven and stumbling. I feel my entire body lifted and tossed over his shoulder like a sack of coffee beans. My fingers cling tightly to his smelly shirt as he clumps down the stairs and throws me into his car.

The car rattles all the way to the city dump, which I recognize by the smell. But this time we're not there to deliver bags of garbage.

"You're on your own now, bastard," he says as he grabs me by the ankles and heaves me out. The door slams and the car roars away.

I sit for a long time on an overturned rusted bucket, a few tears staining it further. I never see my mother or stepfather again.

Guns, guns: used by most of the gang leaders who found, fed, and worked me after that. Used by the thugs and police who wanted us street kids eliminated. But I forbid my group of kids to have any. Way too easy for a pistol in a child's hand to get turned on him, as I witnessed more than once.

• • •

The island gringo's smile dims when he figures out I'm not interested in his air gun. He slides it back into place beside an impressive collection of barbells that explain his muscles. (Ha: push-ups and pull-ups on the yacht's furniture work just as well for me.) Then he leads me to a garage behind the house.

"This bike is Mom's. Your size." He offers a dusty bicycle while throwing his leg over a shiny model with a gazillion gears. (*Gazillion* is my newest English word.)

"Thanks!" I remember to say with enthusiasm. A zing of excitement convinces me I can somehow operate the thing.

Be his friend for the morning, the captain has ordered. Make sure the two of you don't attract any attention and duck any questions or make up answers.

How to act like a friend? I have never had any. None I could trust, anyway. I laugh as my sea legs try to remember how to ride a bike. Then, twisting and turning down a blacktop road between a gazillion trees taller than I have ever seen, I sniff the fresh smells the rain is creating and see some wild deer and fawns.

The wind bounces pine cones off our bicycles while a soft carpet of pine needles and small branches crunches under our tires. I laugh at the splashes on my legs as we plough through storm puddles. Couldn't care less about the mud spatters the bike kicks up or the soaking my clothes are taking.

I have a pinprick memory of my mother teaching me to ride a kids' bike that she "borrowed" from where it was sitting on the mown lawn of some rich people. Several months later someone "borrowed" it from us. But we had it long enough for me to shed the training wheels. And I rode one or two bikes after that to run "errands" for my "protectors." I'm pleased to find that my body still knows how to keep a bike on the road.

Listening to Owen's tales of going to school on a nearby island, I take care to look sympathetic when the boy complains about what strikes me as a perfect life. Soon my companion pauses at the edge of a field with an electric fence.

"Ruffian!" he shouts, taunting a bull bigger than anything I have seen hoofing it down the street during annual running-of-the-bulls festivals. The bull lifts its head like it is a major effort in this windstorm. His nose features a copper ring. Windblown branches from surrounding trees litter his grazing area.

"Ruffian's the most dangerous thing on the island," Owen says, mimicking the bull's snorting.

As I study a barn on the far side of the field, I imagine sprinting across the pasture and hiding in the prickly hay pile inside until Captain pulls up anchor and leaves. Ruffian could protect me throughout the search.

But Captain would not leave, and things would not end well for Ruffian or me. Plus, Captain would never trust me again, which I would pay for big time. No, my future is with our boat, *Archimedes*. And learning more English from our clients.

Snort, snort. I join in making bull sounds, slap Owen on the back, and laugh like I am having a great time. Which I really am by the time we have circled around the lighthouse, blown tunes on long blades of grass while watching eagles circle the grey sky overhead, and dangled our legs from sandstone cave ledges above the whipped-up ocean.

Me: laughing. Me: smiling. Me: feeling as safe as the wild deer grazing yards from us. If my mother is still alive and thinks of me sometimes, she'd like seeing me like this. I mentally download a selfie and send it to her. I wish I could download my life into this place, but …

Soon we are back at the cabin.

"Want to play ring toss?" Owen asks.

"What is?" I'm determined to learn it fast, whatever it is.

The island boy grins as he leads me to a storage shed and points to a stack of life ring buoys. I follow his lead in grabbing a few and toting them outside to where a series of pegs has been pounded into the ground, each labelled with a number: 5, 10, 15, 20, 25, 30, and 35.

"Thirty feet," Owen declares, pointing to the second-to-last peg. "That's my best distance so far. I'm working on nailing thirty-five."

His life ring sails toward the target peg like he is playing horseshoes or tossing a Frisbee.

Wham! The ring hits its mark and stops dead.

"Nice," I say. However silly a game this is, the guy sure has a steady aim.

Owen smiles. "Your turn. Call your peg first."

"Twenty," I decide and flick my wrist to put the ring into the air. It lands short. I hide a frown.

"Good arm muscle, but you need more practice," Owen rules and spends the next twenty minutes coaching me as we play the strange game. Hmm, maybe I will introduce this sport to the captain. I chuckle at the thought, since it will never happen.

Owen laughs like he is pleased to hear me chuckling. "You like Horton Island?"

"Is cool," I reply, using one of the first English expressions I learned from clients.

"You on vacation with your uncle? It's just the two of you?"

"Yes, vacation." Wouldn't that be nice? Of course, I have never had a vacation in my life, but I am proud I know the word.

"Welcome to Canada."

"Thank you." We jump on our bikes and race up and down hills until Owen pulls up at a white wooden grocery store with flower baskets hanging from the eaves. It is too clean to be real: no garbage all over the place, no broken windows or iron bars on the door, no broken glass or liquor bottles or dogs with mangy skin stretched over their rib cages.

I shiver and draw back as I see a young child approaching a Dumpster at the rear of the store.

"You okay?" Owen asks.

I grit my teeth and pull my eyes away. The boy is just tossing something in, I tell myself. There are no armed security guards scowling from the door, no one aiming a gun at him. In fact, nobody else around at all except a smiling man in a yellow raincoat unlocking the front door.

The contrast with Guatemala City makes me feel as if I am dreaming. I have hardly been off *Archimedes* in three years. I shake my head in wonder. "Paradise Island," I mutter.

Owen hoots at that. "For a day, yes. Especially when it's not raining." Then he grows serious. "But my parents forced me to move here. All my friends are in Ontario. All my ex-friends," he corrects himself. Then, in a darker, lower voice, he adds, "And my brother."

Even if I am posing as his friend for the morning, I decide not to ask what all that means.

CHAPTER FOUR

OWEN

After we've eaten lunch in a rain-pounded park picnic shelter, peeked through the windows of some cabins, filled Arturo's packs with stuff from the grocery and hardware stores, and ducked out of the rain into a bird blind on a little pond, my new friend says, "Is time to return to boat."

"Really?" I object from where I'm lying, stomach down, on the worn wood floor of the blind. He has seemed tense ever since the grocery store cashier asked me, "Who's your friend?"

Before I could reply, Arturo told the guy, "We go to high school together." Then he winked at me like we'd agreed on this alibi. Alibi? Why did we need a story? But okay, I'd decided, Arturo was more fun than I'd thought.

"It's only three thirty," I argue. "And the wind and rain are starting to let up."

Arturo squints at the sky. "Will be dark early."

"Yes. But you won't go till morning, will you?"

He shrugs. "Captain decide."

"You mean your uncle."

"Yes, uncle."

As silence hangs between us, a blue heron lands on the pond and flicks its wings to shake off the rain.

"Arturo," I whisper, "think your uncle would let me hitch a ride with you to whatever island you're going to next? I need to get out of here, and it'd be fun to hang out with you more." Sure I've got marina duties, but to heck with them!

My new friend locks his eyes on the heron. I catch amusement on his face. And he takes his time to answer.

"Sounds cool. I need friend on boat. We ask Captain, okay?"

His eyes still on the bird, he reaches out and pats me on the back. A little awkwardly, like he doesn't pat people on the back very often.

If the people on board seem okay, go for it.

They're okay, Gregor. He even said he needs a friend. And you know I damned well do.

A shrill whistle makes me jump. It's a warning screech from the blue heron as it lifts up and flaps away. *Whap, whap, whap.* Dagger beak, bulging throat, dual-colored wings, and spindly legs rise along with the throaty cry.

"Awesome," says Arturo, pronouncing it like a word he has learned only recently, and he's grinning a 100-percent-genuine grin. Which makes me stoked to have brought him here.

"What's your favourite bird?" I ask.

"Hmm ... eagle. Is biggest. You?"

"Raven. It's smarter than an eagle. And even if it's a little smaller, it chases eagles away by ganging up with other ravens."

"Oh." A branch creaks as a turkey vulture lands and perches on it. Arturo makes a face at it.

"Turkey vultures are really big," I say, "but they're nowhere near as respected as eagles or ravens, 'cause their claws are smaller. In the bird world, it's all about talon size. And vultures are greedy. They eat way more than they can handle when they find something dead to binge on. Know what they do if someone interrupts them?"

Arturo shakes his head.

"They make themselves vomit so they're light enough to fly away."

"Gross." Arturo cracks a smile.

I laugh.

• • •

"Here they are! Right on time!" Captain Jones greets us as we shuffle along the dock with our packs full of purchases. "Did you have fun? Get everything? See anyone?"

"*Nadie importante*," Arturo informs him.

I guess at the meaning: *no one important.*

"Coffee in a minute. Come on board," the captain invites me.

43

Yes! Down the companionway and into the galley. It's spacious and stunning, just like the Hans Christian Independence 45 back in Ontario that was named *The Otter*. I help Arturo store the groceries in cupboards and the full-sized stainless steel refrigerator while he and the captain exchange rapid-fire Spanish. Seems like an awful lot of food for two people, even for a long journey. Maybe they're picking up other people soon?

The yacht brings back memories of *The Otter*, which Gregor and I used to play on when Dad wasn't around and there were no customers at the Toronto Marina. Back then, the marina was our backyard, park, and playground, and *The Otter* was owned by an elderly man who never came around. The keys hung in Dad's office. So it was our favourite personal play space for years. We started out playing hide and seek on it. As we grew older, we pretended to operate it, and later, *The Otter* was the boat on which we learned to do tune-ups and repairs. Gregor and I dreamed of taking it out to see the world together.

I know all the mechanics and every nook and cranny of this vessel. Which makes me itch to handle it — just around our little bay for a few minutes. Or to one of the nearby islands that has a ferry back to Horton. So what if I miss school for a day? My parents won't find out. Officer Olsen is used to me going off fishing or overnight camping, so he won't sound an alarm. And Arturo invited me, sort of.

The captain finishes pouring us mugs of coffee, adding cream and sugar to mine without asking. My entire body basks in its flowing warmth. I tell him about our day, and as the storm finally fades, we talk about boats and weather and the region's geography.

"Can I have a tour of *Archimedes*?" I finally ask, my eyes on the lower companionway.

"You mean go below?" The captain exchanges glances with Arturo. "No, Owen. Sorry. I'm ashamed of the mess down there."

"Okay. But maybe I can pilot *Archimedes* for a few minutes before you leave?"

Is Arturo throwing me a warning look? The captain just chuckles. "Not a chance, young man. We're in a hurry to move on tonight."

"Move on to where?"

The friendly expression evaporates. The eyes narrow. Then he forces a wooden grin to his lips. "Just cruising the Strait, Owen. Heading toward Nanaimo, maybe."

"You're leaving tonight? In this weather?"

"Storm going now," Arturo says. "Radio say okay."

"Can I go with you as far as Nanaimo, Captain Jones? I can pay for gas and food and catch a ferry back from there. I won't be any trouble at all."

The captain pulls himself up to his full height, his uncombed hair touching the ceiling of the galley. His freshly shaven face is stern and his voice is loud and clear: "Sorry, Owen. The answer is no."

Arturo throws me a sympathetic look. I struggle to mask a sigh. "Well, I appreciate the coffee. *Hasta la vista* and great to meet you."

They shake my hand; I step off the boat and slump up the steps. Slowly, not even trying to make it a workout.

• • •

You could stow away like we did once, Gregor says when I get to my bedroom and prop his photo up.

"Yeah, but we were kids and that was a customer we knew, who thought it was funny."

So? You know exactly where to hide on that boat.

"I do," I say, and I pull out my wetsuit, water bottle, water purification tablets, and waterproof backpack. Into the last item I stuff my wallet, down parka, rain poncho, some spare clothes, a compass, and a headlamp. I do another quick search for my cellphone, but no luck.

What's with the power? Still not on. Takes forever out here in the boonies. So I sit at our living room window with my binoculars trained on the dock. As night closes in, I can barely see the yacht — just enough to know they're still just hanging out. I'm waiting for signs they're about to head out, or for total dark, whichever comes first. I'll be back long before my parents, so there will be no worry on their part.

As the light fades to near darkness, I stand and stare. A half-dozen seals have surrounded *Archimedes.* They swim around and around the boat, like synchronized swimmers twisting and diving, or like mermaids. Huh?

I push the binoculars harder against my eyes, only to spot the captain on the deck aiming binoculars in my direction. I'm inside with no lights on, so he can't possibly see me. Anyway, I won't be approaching *Archimedes* from our stairs. And the neurotic seals will surely have disappeared by then.

It's well past midnight when a spike of activity makes me suspect *Archimedes* is about to slip anchor. I lower the binoculars, grab my stuff, and lock up the house. Using some absentee neighbour's rickety cliff steps, I slink down to the beach and enter the cold black water.

There's no splashing; the seals have disappeared. Just the soothing *whoosh* of wind-stirred trees, the lapping of water, and the rigging in the masts shivering as the storm blows its last puffs.

Navigating by feel and my senses, ignoring the initial shocking chill, I swim slowly and noiselessly to our dock and then under it. Soon I'm near *Archimedes*'s rear swim platform, the steel-bracketed ledge from which swimmers and divers can lower themselves.

A flashback of pulling myself up that fateful night, my chilled hand gripping Gregor's. I squelch the memory with all my might.

Hiding in the air pocket beneath the ledge for long minutes, I wait until I hear the captain and Arturo go quiet. That's when I lift myself with flat palms and strong biceps onto the swim platform. Pausing to make sure no one has heard me, I push my feet up a ladder leading to where the dinghy hangs from davits — giant metal arms — that extend from the rear upper deck. It's upright and covered.

Ahh. Feels so good to crawl under the tarpaulin, wriggle out of my wetsuit and into dry clothes from my waterproof backpack, wrap myself in my down parka and rain poncho, and settle myself on the rubber floor. Like lying in a comfy cradle.

I can't see the stars when they come out, but the gentle sway of my bed as *Archimedes* heads out puts me to sleep fast, content in the belief that in the morning, they'll welcome me aboard after a brief scolding.

• • •

ARTURO

While the customers have their weekly night swim, it's my job to wash their clothes and scrub down their quarters. I toss their smelly belongings into a heap, slipping my hand into pockets to transfer the odd coin to my own pockets.

At one point, I pause to run my fingers over the gold monogram embroidered on one of their blazers and slip my feet into one of the pairs of thick-soled leather shoes that I polish and line up for them daily. Just for a second, I let myself dream of being a rich schoolboy, of speaking English so well I can apply for a job as a guide on a tour boat. Or maybe I'd just buy a boat and cruise around the world. I would fill it with lots of food and give rides to kids who have never been on a boat.

The stench of an unflushed head quickly yanks me back to reality. They may have a life they take for granted, but I love my job, I try to convince myself as I apply mop to floor and pump out and wipe down the overflowing toilet basin. I steer my mind to the pay Captain will give me when we reach our destination in a day or two, and I smile.

This is my second trip up the coast this year, and it's not even June yet. The little tin that holds my savings is growing heavier. It guards against my gnawing fear of ending up hungry and back on the streets. I may not deserve this awesome job, but I will do absolutely anything it takes to keep it.

Thump, thump. Six naked, half-frozen bodies scramble back onto *Archimedes* and elbow each other to stampede down the stairs to the second stateroom, the one the captain doesn't sleep in. Each boy holds one of the small threadbare towels the captain has assigned them.

"Where'd you put our clothes, you bonehead?" demands a shivering Danillo, the boy I work hardest to avoid.

"Yeah, you'd better not be stealing from us again!" says sumo-wrestler-sized Sebastian, also in Spanish, of course.

"The head is disgusting," accuses Sergio, Sebastian's twin, who is equally impressive in size. "You need to clean it more often."

"And stop stealing from our food rations. Think we're stupid or something?" adds Lucas, the one with expensive-looking, thick glasses.

Everyone is quivering with cold and digging in duffle bags to locate their clean clothes. They have two sets each.

What, not posh enough for you? I want to say. *Want me to ask Captain to upgrade you to first class? Or maybe we can toss you off the ship to improve our ballast?*

But the thoughts pass as quickly as I walk away with mop in motion and teeth gritted. Showing feelings is a weakness that brings on trouble. Messing with rich boys increases the risk big time. These are lessons I learned before I could walk. But the clients aren't finished with me yet.

"Arturo the kiss-ass," Danillo says, stalking over to put his face up to mine. I step a little to the left and lower my hand to where I keep my pocket knife. Not that I'd ever use it on a client.

"Captain's pet. Arturo the Artful Dodger," Danillo continues with the menacing smile that makes my chest start prickling with an electrical charge. He has switched to English, which he assumes I can't understand well. It's the language all the boys use amongst themselves, because they come from a Guatemala City private school that allows only English. "But of course, you wouldn't know about the Artful Dodger."

The other boys laugh. I pull my face into a neutral mask, lower my shoulders and look away. I mentally lower the buzz in my body. There's a certain power in doing the invisible servant act, in not reacting to their taunts. But someday …

"The Artful Dodger is a character in *Oliver Twist*, a book about a pickpocket scumbag like you. But don't think you can dodge us forever, you nasty little thief —"

"Arturo!" the captain shouts from the salon above. "Finish up and get your bony butt up here *pronto*. And tell the customers to find their accommodations, or I'll be down to speed things up."

The deep-voiced Spanish, followed by a shrill blast from the whistle around the captain's neck, sends the boys scurrying. Hopping one-legged as they pull on trousers, they dive into the storage cupboards and bulkhead lockers, which are in the dividing walls.

I smile at the suddenly empty and quiet second stateroom and amble up the companionway to my boss.

An hour later, I am curled up in my sleeping bag on the cushions around the eating nook when I think I hear a soft bump on the swim platform. Probably just an adventurous otter. I'm way too tired to go look.

CHAPTER FIVE

OWEN

It's morning and my limbs feel like drumsticks tossed into a freezer. My empty stomach is mewling like a sea lion. I'm ready to crawl out of the dinghy except for the yelling going on down in the salon. The clash of voices could make a dude imagine it's coming from more than two people.

"Arturo!" the captain shouts again, followed by a bunch of angry Spanish. I wince for my friend as I wonder what the hell he has done to make his uncle so mad. But minutes later it's quiet, and the smell of something frying tempts me to leave my hideout. Refried beans, if my nostrils have it right. Definitely time to make my move.

I stretch under the cover of my tarpaulin and lace on my boots. Stashing my stuff in the dinghy, I poke my head out and climb down the ladder to the stern deck. As I stroll past a window with a smirk on my face and "Surprise!" on my tongue, I find my greeting drowned out by a single startling whistle blast.

"Hey!" I say, stepping over the door stoop of the aft deck. "Guess who stowed away on *Archimedes* last night?"

The captain freezes in place, an astonished and angry glare on his face. His fork clatters to his plate, and a silver whistle on a cord around his neck drops from his mouth. Why did he blow the whistle just now? His knees push him halfway up from his seat in the eating alcove. Next thing I know, his right hand dives under the table, like he's grabbing at his lower pant leg.

Just as fast, Arturo places a restraining hand on his uncle's arm. His open-mouthed surprise changes to a shaky smile.

"Owen!"

He's standing between the captain and the galley, holding a heavy iron frying pan. For a split second, despite his smile, I wonder if he's going to hurl it at me.

"Hi, Captain. Hi, Arturo," I say a little less confidently than intended. "Sorry to surprise you. But I really, really wanted a ride on *Archimedes*. Only to the next port, wherever you're going. So I snuck on last night and — hey, who's on lookout if you two are here?" It occurs to me that I've heard them talking and yelling for a good fifteen minutes in the salon.

Arturo lays down the frying pan, exchanges glances with the captain, and dashes up the companionway to the pilothouse.

"Captain," he calls down, and finishes the sentence in Spanish. I figure he's reassuring the captain that it's fine for me to be here.

The captain's stormy face struggles to change expression. His arm relaxes and comes up from under the table. He takes fork in hand again and plunges it into his beans and cheese.

"So, you're a sneaky little marina rat, are you? When did you join us? And where did you sleep?" he asks over-solicitously with sharp, not-so-friendly eyes.

"After dark," I say, head lowered. "I slept in the dinghy. Hey, I'll swab decks and pump heads and all that stuff to pay my way. Just needed a change of scene, you know? A little adventure." With Gregor, who told me to come pick him up.

"Do your parents know where you are going? Does anyone?" he demands in that bass voice.

"No one," I admit.

His face softens slightly and he devours the last of the breakfast on his plate. "Okay, then. You're our guest till next port. That'll be in a couple of hours," he says in an overloud voice, as if to make sure Arturo and anyone within a mile hears. "Hungry?"

"Starved!" I reply with a big grin.

"Arturo! Get down here and rustle up some breakfast for our stowaway. I'll take the controls now." With that, he rises and lopes off. I wonder how long they leave the helm unmanned. Even on an automated luxury craft like this, it should never be for more than ten minutes at a time.

• • •

ARTURO

This is not good at all, I reflect, cracking some eggs for Owen. I hope Captain can find a port fast, and get in and out even faster.

And yet, why does it secretly amuse me to see the captain rattled and to imagine the clients holed up — cramped, silent, and anxious — with their stomachs rumbling for my good grub? Especially Danillo, who had to abandon his pilothouse watch and dive into the storage drawer under the two-seater behind the captain's seat when the whistle blew. Probably got himself some bruises and is running out of good breathing air. I smile wider.

Hah! It is a pleasant change of routine, and Owen is someone new to practise my English with. Even someone to help me with chores. Anyway, it is only for a few hours.

"Over easy with bacon?" I ask, pronouncing Danillo's favourite command with as little accent as possible.

"How'd you know?" Owen responds with a broad grin.

"What kind of jam you like on your toast?"

"Raspberry. Maybe you have some orange juice, too? I can get it from the fridge."

"Sure," I respond. "Help yourself." This boy is way more polite than the clients. Keep him busy. Keep him in sight.

"So this is one nice rig for just the two of you." Owen is peering around with his arm slung over the back of the eight-seat, horseshoe-shaped galley sofa. He looks all too at home.

"Two staterooms, right? And this nook converts to a bed. Altogether, I'm guessing *Archimedes* sleeps seven, parties thirty-five," he quips like he has read the website.

"It is awesome," I say, mimicking Pequeño (Spanish for *little*), my favourite client on this run, the youngest of the bunch at eleven. The toast pops up; I butter it and deliver the breakfast to the "marina rat," a new phrase to add to my English vocabulary.

"What do we have for chores this morning?" Owen asks as he digs in. "I'm a hard worker, you know."

"Owen?" the captain calls from the bridge a few minutes later as Owen and I finish washing the breakfast dishes.

Owen runs up the companionway and I move to the bottom of the stairs to listen in. Captain has his nautical charts spread out, and he questions the island boy about various ports and ocean currents without revealing where exactly we're heading. Even I do not know our destination for sure, since it changes on some trips. Owen answers Captain's questions easily, like he really knows the region.

"Can I take the wheel for a minute?" I hear him ask eagerly.

"Sure," says Captain.

We need to keep this boy aboard. He makes Captain stay nice.

Captain lets Owen run *Archimedes* for a few minutes while I put away the dishes and drift back to spy on them. I love spying.

"Shall I hold it at twenty five hundred rpm or maintain eight knots?" Owen asks like he has operated this kind of boat before. Took me months to learn my way around *Archimedes*. I remember Captain training me, sometimes patiently, sometimes boxing me around the ears. I was a fast learner. I took to the sea like a seal pup. Now running a yacht is my world. It feels like the island boy lives in the same world.

"Hold it at twenty five hundred rpm." Captain answers Owen, with a hint of surprise.

"Is the autohelm set on the correct course?"

"You bet."

"Engine temperature seems to be fine. Oil pressure is good."

"Arturo!" Captain snaps, catching me on the lower landing. "To your chores!"

At this, Owen leaps up. "I promised to help him."

"No need —" Captain starts, but Owen has already dashed down the companionway and opened the closet holding the buckets, mops, and brushes. How did he know where that was, I wonder, exchanging a worried look with Captain.

"No you open doors without my permission, slave," I try to joke.

"Gotcha," Owen replies with a salute. He grabs some window cleaner and a roll of paper towels, heads down the lower companionway, and starts in on a mirror in the nearest head. So I squirt some cleaner into the sink beside him and begin scrubbing.

We laugh as we bump elbows. We speed up like we are in a race and we chat about *Archimedes*'s features as we move from one task to another.

"Why's it called *Archimedes*?"

"Is famous owl in movie. Captain likes owls."

"Yeah? Owls are sneaky. Their special feathers let them fly silently in the night. But they can't see what's going on around them without swivelling their heads back and forth. And they eat smaller owls. That's mean, huh? They use their talons to crush the skull and body."

"You know much about birds," I say, impressed and amused.

Owen and I move into the main cabin, the captain's private room with its queen-size bed and patchwork quilt. This is awesome, big time. We are going to finish chores in record time.

"What's with the whistle around your neck?" Owen asks.

Think fast. "For soccer games Captain and I play in salon," I joke.

"Yeah, right." Owen waits.

"Is special bird caller. Brings birds if we are near shore."

"Sure." Owen smirks.

I spot some dead flies in the globe of the light over the captain's bed. Stepping up onto the mattress, I lean back to unscrew and clean it.

My whistle dangles down my back. I never imagine that Owen will leap up onto the bed beside me, grab it, and blast it twice.

CHAPTER SIX

OWEN

It was just a joke. I didn't blow it hard, not even hard enough for the captain to hear from the pilothouse.

What I don't expect is for Arturo to spin around, lock his arms around my neck, and tackle me to the bed. The air whooshes out of my lungs and my fingers clutch the flannel quilt. Then comes the creak of cupboard and bulkhead doors flying open and the heart-stopping sight of three boys spilling out. Body odour and curiosity waft through the air as they stand around the bed, staring at us.

"Who's he?" asks a tall, skinny one.

"Shut up," Arturo says in English between clenched teeth. Then he delivers orders in excited Spanish that include the word *capitán* along with gestures toward the closet doors. Clearly, he wants them to disappear into the cupboards again before the captain comes.

It occurs to me that I could easily elbow Arturo hard

and free myself, but there's no predicting what these guys might do then. *Who the hell are they, anyway?*

"No way!" says a giant one, hands on his hips. "We're hungry, and he has already seen us. Who are you?" he addresses me directly. There's a Hispanic accent, but all three boys have much lighter skin and accents than Arturo. And they're dressed in identical trousers and white dress shirts. The skinny one even wears a blazer and tie. How dorky is that?

"Who are *you*?" I manage, despite my squeezed throat. "Arturo, let up."

He relaxes his hold a little, but not enough to release me. And he keeps turning his head toward the door. No captain appears. There are no shouts from above. Finally he rolls off my stunned body, motions one of the boys to shut the door, and faces me.

"These are clients," Arturo says. "They play hide and seek. Now you spoil the game."

So two whistle blasts is a signal, obviously, but it still doesn't add up. Illegal immigrants? Hopefully not, or else I've landed myself in a wasp's nest. I remain speechless as I rub my neck.

The boys' eyes bore into me. All three are my age, or maybe a little younger.

"He is a stowaway," Arturo says, finally breaking the silence. "We exit him off soon." His face is rigid with fear and anger.

"Not 'exit.' You mean drop him off, Arturo," says the skinny one. "Cool. Are you Canadian? I'm Gabriel."

"Hi Gabriel. Where are you from?" I ask. "I'm Owen."

The first mate gives me dagger eyes between glances toward the door, as though a murderous pirate is about to burst in. He speaks sharply to the boys in Spanish, gesturing again to their hiding places and jerking his head once toward me. They laugh and wave him off.

"Breakfast, Arturo! We want our breakfast!"

"Your funeral," he mumbles, and, with his head low, he walks out of the room, shutting the door softly behind him.

"We're from Guatemala City," says Gabriel.

"We all go to a private boys' school there," says the first large boy.

"Where we're not allowed to speak anything but English," says the other large one I'm guessing is the other's twin.

"Yeah, so we speak English all the time," says the first twin, "especially 'cause Arturo can't understand us much. He's the captain's slave. Captain is mean, but we're almost at where we're going, so we don't have to put up with him and the Artful Dodger much longer. That's what we call Arturo. He dodges Captain's fists sometimes."

There's some half-hearted laughter at that. My brain wallows like a stalled boat in heavy fog as it attempts to process thoughts.

"Been holed up on this stupid boat for more than two weeks," adds Gabriel.

"And we miss our families," says a twin.

"Tell us about Canada! Where do you live? What's your school like?" they ask.

"Is everyone rich?"

"What do Canadians eat?"

"Are there really wild bears around here?"

"You're not a spy or a cop, are you?"

This question prompts shivers down my back. Please don't be illegal immigrants.

"'Cause we don't like spies or cops."

Okay, ostrich-brain, pull your melon out of the sand. It's all starting to make sense. No wonder Arturo wanted me to stay away from the "clients." Of course the captain would have wanted to get rid of me quickly. And now it's obvious why there is so much fuel and food, and why the Artful Dodger was dodging questions.

"Where is Captain dropping you off, anyway?" Gabriel asks.

"Captain is dropping him off in Nanaimo in a couple of hours," comes a gruff voice as a boot flings the door open. "And you lot had better be at the table in three seconds or I'll feed your breakfast and you to the sea lions."

I'm still recovering from the shock of sharing the boat with a couple of uniformed schoolboys as the captain grins and pats me on the back. "Well, Owen, you surprised us, and now we've surprised you. Welcome to our school cruise. I hope you enjoy their company till we reach Nanaimo. They're a fun group, really. But too old for hide and seek, seems to me."

Got that right. He's not fooling me, but I'll play along for now.

He chuckles and guides me back up to the salon. "Arturo says you two finished up the cleaning already. Well done. Back to the bridge with me, then?"

"Um, sure," I say, since the large hand pressed against my back is steering me there firmly.

"*Hola*, Owen!" the boys greet me from where they're grouped around the eating nook, being handed plates by a stressed-looking Arturo. I regard him a little warily.

The number of schoolboys has grown from three to four. As in, another one must have been hiding upstairs.

"This is Lucas. And I'm Sergio. My twin brother is Sebastian."

"Hi," I say, wondering how many more haven't come out yet. *Sleeps seven, parties thirty-five*, as the ads say. They introduce themselves to me as the smell of eggs and bacon wafts from the stove.

"No need to remember names," the captain says with a wink as he continues to guide me up to the bridge. There, a tall, muscled boy is on lookout. He turns from the wheel and gives me a full once-over, like a customs guard inspecting me before ruling whether or not I can enter the country.

"Danillo," he says abruptly, shaking my hand firmly. Then he turns back to the controls. "Alter heading fifteen degrees port for deadhead."

I look where he indicates and see the log travelling vertically in the current. Deadheads can do serious damage if not identified and avoided. Well spotted, I think.

I glance at the radio and have to use all my self-control to stop from reaching for it. I need to call Officer Olsen and tell him I've discovered a boatful of illegals. *Oh, and by the way, please rescue me since I've managed to be dumb-assed enough to land myself in the middle of them.*

"Got it. Go get your breakfast," the captain says to Danillo.

"Okay." Danillo's long legs take two steps at a time down the companionway.

The other boys stop talking as he enters the galley.

"Eggs over easy," he commands Arturo.

• • •

ARTURO

"You let him blow your whistle?" Captain booms at me while the boys are in the stateroom talking with the stowaway. His right palm flies out from nowhere and slaps my cheek hard. I put my hand up to where it stings and back away a step, squelching the electrical current that says to fight back. Danillo turns his face toward the water and does his best to pretend we're not there as he pilots the boat.

The same large hand balls itself into a fist and punches me full force in the gut.

"Uhh," my chest responds as the wind goes out of it and I slump into the seat behind Danillo.

"Now I have to get down there and separate them from the boy, you useless piece of trash!"

As he exits the pilothouse two steps ahead of me, I'm hoping his moment of violence is done. Maybe I deserve it. I shouldn't have taken Owen down when he blew my whistle, but I can't change that now. The boys should have known better than to come out, whistle or no, with a stranger's voice aboard. They're too naive like that.

As I serve breakfast, Captain steers the stowaway up to the pilothouse and the boys chatter in the eating area.

"Arturo, bring me a muffin," Sebastian calls out as he seats himself at the table.

"Arturo, where'd you put the Monopoly game? Stop moving things around and help me find it!" Gabriel whines.

It's how they always treat me, but I feel my face burn knowing the Canadian boy can hear it all. And from the pilothouse, I hear Captain's voice. "Owen, it's a privilege to have such a skilled lad at the helm." Like he's some kind of visiting prince.

I pause to watch Sergio reading a fat English book I couldn't tackle even if it was in Spanish while slurping down the orange juice I just made him on command, spilling some on the white dress shirt I'll now need to wash and iron.

Arturo, these muffins you made are amazing.

Arturo, come eat with us at the table for once.

Arturo, put down your mop and join us for Monopoly. We need another player.

Arturo, thanks for getting that stain out of my jeans yesterday, and I can't believe you ironed them too.

If only. In the real world, they talk to me only when they need something, and Captain allows me to eat only their leftovers, and never at the table; he keeps a log of all food and locks the fridge at night. They speak English to keep me out of their conversations, and they look at my tattered jeans like …

I pull my thoughts away to the new worry. Things could go bad fast if any of the boys lets anything slip before *Archimedes* drops off our stowaway. I check my watch and relax a little. Less than an hour. Does Owen suspect what *Archimedes* is really all about? There's no sign he does.

"More coffee!" Sergio demands. I imagine spilling a little on his wrist as I pour, but it's only a stray thought. Besides, I have had enough grief for one morning.

"Chess, anyone?" Danillo calls out as he pushes his breakfast plate away and stretches his hands over his head, feet up on the cushions. He looks at everyone but me.

No one can beat Danillo at chess, so no one volunteers immediately. But we all jump when Owen comes charging down the companionway, ignoring the Captain's calls to come back.

"Chess?" he echoes in an enthusiastic voice. "I'm game."

Hands on his hips at the top of the companionway, Captain glares at me like it is my fault the stowaway is mixing with the clients. But as he watches the two set up the board, he shrugs and turns back to the bridge.

I clear dishes and wipe the table, invisible as a ghost to the boys pressed around the chess players.

Wait, only five schoolboys? One is missing. The one nicknamed Pequeño, my favourite. Barely eleven, he spends most of his time sleeping or reading comic books by flashlight in his special hiding place, as if he's half afraid of the older boys. Well, that's for the best till after we reach Nanaimo.

CHAPTER SEVEN

OWEN

Danillo is an ace chess player, but so am I. At first he holds himself stiffly, but eventually he relaxes and a smile appears. Pretty soon we're chatting between moves. Chess is a good way to distract myself from thoughts of the situation I seem to have gotten myself into.

The game encourages the boys pressed around us to talk, too, and in no time we're one big party discussing everything from what a drag homework is to what kinds of storms *Archimedes* has been through on the way up here. But there's some info they seem to be avoiding. No way am I going to ask them any more questions about why they're visiting Canada on a "school cruise."

"Your dad owns a yacht?" I ask Danillo after over-hearing one of the other boys' comments.

"He did. That's why I get asked to help out a little on *Archimedes*. But Arturo knows way more," he adds, frowning.

Jealous, I muse. Not that you'd ever know from the way he bosses Arturo around.

"Danillo, can I play next?" asks one of the boys hanging over us.

"No, get lost," Danillo replies.

"Danillo, is it okay to turn on some music?"

"Danillo, Sergio is hogging the sofa. Tell him to move."

"You seem to be the leader of this bunch," I observe.

"Bunch of hooligans," he replies. "Guys, give us a break. Owen's the guest of honour. *Madre de Dios!* You nabbed my queen!" He scratches his head. "Who'd you learn chess from, Kasparov?"

"Sure, on a chess scholarship to Russia," I deadpan.

"Really?" asks Sebastian, one of the bouncer-sized twins.

"I live on a boring island with no friends. Not much to do but play chess online," I explain.

"Arturo!" the captain shouts. I'd almost forgotten Arturo existed. He scurries up the companionway to his uncle.

Danillo stares after them, frowning.

"Checkmate," I declare.

He turns back to me. "I surrender," he mumbles with a half grin, then he leaves the table to hover below and just out of sight of the captain and his first mate, who are talking urgently in hushed Spanish.

"What're they saying?" I whisper, joining Danillo.

"Boat following us. Coming too close," he translates for me.

I start to move up the companionway when the captain's shrill whistle sounds. Danillo grabs my arms and pulls me down the lower companionway. "Follow me," he orders huskily.

By the time we reach the lower deck, the boys are disappearing. They leap into every nook and cranny on the boat like they've got assigned places and have done this a hundred times before.

Illegal immigrants whisked into and out of hiding. Brilliant.

Danillo and I run down to the second stateroom, where we crouch just below a porthole. My heart starts doing gymnastics. Peering out, fingers clutching the bottom rim of the porthole, we watch an eighteen-foot, Defender-class, rigid-hulled inflatable approach. At the helm is a grey-bearded man in a bulky coat and large felt hat. A green weathered tarp fills the other half of the boat.

"Can you help me?" he's calling to the captain.

Grey-bearded man. Officer Olsen's *WANTED* poster.

"Stay back. Don't come alongside!" booms the captain in response.

"But I need help and you're the only one around," the man insists, gliding the rigid hull raft toward us at a speed that makes me brace for collision.

"Back away!" the captain orders.

Danillo and I duck as pistol shots fire from *Archimedes*'s bridge. The captain's got a gun. The Defender only seems to speed up. As it touches our bow, the operator jumps up — his fake beard sagging as one of its straps snaps off — and four brawny men rise from under the tarp and leap aboard with him, small machine guns in their hands.

My pulse does triple time. The captain's gun clatters to the deck.

"Hide!" Danillo urges, trying to push me into the head.

But I know a better place. I sprint to the captain's stateroom, open up the double cupboard doors above the head of the bed, and crawl up into the chain locker, which I know has space for more than chains.

There, I lift a tarp to hide under — only to find another person there. A small one, shaking.

"Hey, I'm not going to hurt you, kid," I whisper. "But play dead. We've got robbers on board."

"R-r-robbers? I-I'm scared. Who are you?" he whispers.

"Owen. Friend of Arturo's," I decide to say. "Shh."

"I'm Pequeño," he whispers, so I can hardly hear him. And after a long pause, "Everyone hates Arturo but me."

There's shouting right over our heads, the *tat-a-tat* of a machine gun, and the thump of bodies hitting the deck.

"I'll be right back," I promise Pequeño. Pulse throbbing, I wriggle onward from the chain locker into the engine room, where I find a ceiling hatch to raise a crack.

One of the intruders is pressing the captain's face into the deck. Only feet away, I spot the prone body of Arturo beside him. Holy shit. What should I do?

I watch a pirate tie the big man's hands and feet while resting a boot on his neck and pointing an Uzi in his face. The captain barks something in Spanish. As Arturo's hoarse voice responds, I shake with relief. At least he's still alive.

"Uhh!" The captain shouts in pain as a second man applies a swift boot to his rib cage.

"The safe!" the man orders, kicking him again.

The captain and Arturo exchange more words, the tone between them growing angrier. Finally, two men hoist Arturo up like an injured dog and drag him to a steel box that clearly needs a key to be opened.

They're making Arturo open the safe, I realize. Maybe it's a simple robbery, and after they steal money they'll take off and leave us alone. I don't want to think about what could go down if they discover the school-boys or me. Maybe I should've stayed home on boring Horton Island after all.

With a creak of a hinge, the safe door is opened, and Arturo gets tossed back to the deck with bruising force. As two of the men scoop the contents out and into a burlap sack, two others head for the companionway.

Quickly, I lower the hatch and crawl back to Pequeño.

"W-what's going on?" he asks.

I relate what I've seen and extend my hand in the dark to pat his head, but find myself brushing his wet face instead.

"If they find us they'll arrest Captain and Arturo and send us home," he whimpers.

"Bandits don't arrest —" I wince as I hear a thump and then Arturo screaming out in pain.

"But Coast Guard ..." Pequeño stops.

"The Coast Guard doesn't rob —" Then I fall silent. *Stop playing dumb, Owen. Too late for that.*

I lean closer to Pequeño. "Is the captain Arturo's uncle?"

A guffaw bursts through his nose. "No."

"And you're not on a school cruise?"

The same snort. "We're moving to Canada. Our parents paid lots of money to get us here. If the robbers steal the money, Captain is going to get really, really mean."

"So he's a coyote. A snakehead. A people smuggler."

This time, it's Pequeño who shushes me, like he's bored with my stupid questions.

There's a small cavalcade of footsteps, like an army is spreading out through *Archimedes*. My body stiffens as hard as steel. There's pushing, a ruckus of shouts, the opening and slamming of doors, all while Arturo and the captain screech at the invaders. Finally, the clatter of boot-falls feeds back onto the deck. A volley of shots (I'm hoping into the air) is punctuated by a victorious cry from the strangers as they push off in their boat — felt by Pequeño and me as a sudden jerk to port.

The sound of a motor, fading laughter, then silence.

"I'll be back," I say again to Pequeño and hustle to my peeping hatch.

On the deck, there's an ugly wrestling match going on. One large captain is freeing his tied-up first mate between also punching him, and one first mate is releasing the captain's bonds while trying to duck the blows.

Finally, both free, they stumble to their feet. The captain unbuckles his belt and lets its buckle end fly. Arturo winces as it hits him — so do I. He attempts to run away, but his boss's hooked elbow closes around his neck and tosses him easily to the deck again.

I feel my jaw tighten as the captain proceeds to whip the shit out of Arturo, who looks all too practised at rolling into a ball and protecting his head with his arms.

"Stop it!" I shout, lifting the hatch cover and leaping up to my curled-up friend.

I reach him in time to see the captain's hand raised and a full contingent of schoolboy witnesses behind him, their heads moving from the open, empty safe to the scene in front of them. Something about the expression on their faces makes me think they've seen the captain beating his employee before.

The captain's hand lowers. The belt slides back around his big waist.

"Get the hell out of my sight, all of you!" he roars.

The boys back up quickly, all but Pequeño, who is staring at Arturo with a trembling lip.

"Help me, Pequeño," I say, my hands on Arturo's welt-covered arms.

• • •

ARTURO

They got all the money, but did not find anyone. They would have killed Captain and me if Captain had not caved. He told me where the key to the safe was when they had him hog-tied with a gun in his face. Now it suits the big man to deny it. For the favour of saving Captain, me, and the boys, I get a beating.

Belt leather slices into my back like electric shocks. I feel welts rise and sting like hot coals. I bite my tongue, roll into a ball, and refuse to make a sound. Again and again come the needle-sharp slaps. Previous scars offer pads of protection, while hits on my unscarred skin rip the flesh like sharp fingernails. But the swats to my unhealed skin are the worst, like pressing salt into an open wound.

As I count to ten, I forgive him because I have no choice, and because I know how he grew up: with violent parents no different than my stepfather and the street-gang leaders of my childhood.

"They pounded me within an inch of my life every week," Captain once told me. "But at least I got their money when they died."

We understand each other. We're from the same world.

Another strike. I hold my breath to keep from crying out. The difference between Captain and me, I remind myself while ignoring the electricity in my body that says to show Captain my own fists, is that he has long since grown into his parents' fists, whereas I vowed never to do that. I swore to be the broken chain. And succeeded with my street kids. Even if I failed them in the end.

The clients think I'm weak, but they don't understand that an occasional session of violence is far easier to take than the piercing pain of hunger and constant fear on the street.

Anyway, who am I to dream of a private schoolboy's life, with all its options? And in the end, what Captain does to me, he is less likely to do to them. *You should thank me, you soft-bellied bastards.*

The session would have gone on longer if not for the brave and stupid interference of the stowaway.

"Stop it!" he orders, standing in front of the silent clients.

"Get the hell out of my sight, all of you!" Captain bellows.

Most of them scatter fast.

I would disappear, too, if I could move. I wince as Owen and Pequeño cup their hands under me and carry me down to the bed in the second stateroom. The only two people on board half safe from Captain's temper.

I gasp as they remove my sweatshirt, press wet cloths to the dried blood, and apply ice to my face and shoulders. I don't fight when they lift my head to help me swallow water and aspirin. But I squeeze my eyes and throat shut, as their kindness threatens to unleash tears.

"Nothing is broken," I mumble. They did not find anyone. They did not kill anyone. And I am just bruised, no broken bones. Three things worth celebrating, if only to myself. They got Captain's gun, but he has another one hidden in the locked drawer of his stateroom.

I struggle to lift myself on one elbow; I need to do chores or ask Captain what I can do. I'm his first mate and he has been robbed. But Captain is not calling me, my attendants are shushing me, and I am starting to drift off.

"Thank you," I mumble to Owen and Pequeño. Then I jerk to attention. Owen. Pequeño. Not a good combination. What has gone down between these two? And what is the stowaway thinking? I look into Owen's face and know he knows. It cancels out the rest of the celebrations and haunts the half sleep I fall into.

CHAPTER EIGHT

OWEN

Our decidedly un-jolly captain steers *Archimedes* into a puddle-size harbour with a less-than-stylin' huddle of buildings. He spends an hour anchored well away from the public dock, whacking away at his keyboard and barking into his cellphone. Clearly just wanting a wireless connection.

The boys sit like concrete statues around the table with pale faces and grim mouths. They don't speak to each other or to me. They don't ask the captain if they can take the dinghy into the village and walk around or get supplies. No one makes coffee or scrounges for food. No one pulls out any of the board games stacked on a shelf.

I spot an atlas and tote it to the table.

"Looking for Nanaimo?" Danillo asks. His nasty tone takes me by surprise.

I turn and look at him.

"None of us is going where we were going," he states, eyes narrowed. "Get over it already, stowaway."

The other boys look away. I dare not ask Danillo what he means. But he has obviously overheard something from the captain's conversations.

Worst-case scenario is that the captain will now see me as trouble. He doesn't know it's probably too early for Officer Olsen or anyone else to sound an alarm on me. But when my officer friend does, the Coast Guard will be on alert, the last thing the captain needs. And he's between a rock and a riptide; if he dumps me alive, I could report his operation. If he doesn't, the search will heat up. Shit. I'm in the mother of all pickle sandwiches.

"Danillo!" comes the captain's shout.

And then Danillo is gone, up to the bridge.

"How's Arturo?" Lucas asks while wiping the lenses of his glasses, but somehow it doesn't sound like he really cares.

"Pequeño is looking after him," I reply before rising and walking toward the lower companionway. If I leave the salon maybe they won't see the sweat that has broken out all over my body.

A glance back reveals the boys huddling closer and speaking in low tones. They've switched to Spanish while I'm within earshot, but it doesn't stop me from detecting the fear in their voices.

When I reappear in the second stateroom, Pequeño nods and heads upstairs to join his schoolmates. Arturo is tossing and turning. His swollen-shut eyelids are purple and blue. His lips are puffed and split.

Dozens of questions crowd my brain, number one being will the captain drop me off somewhere? He doesn't know I know the setup.

Illegal immigrants. Under eighteens, known as minors. And me in the middle of an operation. I wrack my brain for any illegal-immigrant interception stories Officer Olsen has told me. He likes sharing such accounts as much as I like hearing them. And the Canadian Coast Guard gets boatloads of illegals now and then. The coyotes get arrested and the would-be immigrants get processed. Some of the smuggled get permission to stay; some get sent home. It's all pretty orderly and humane. It's rare for the passengers to get hurt or locked up, especially not minors, as far as I know.

That is, if they're lucky enough to get rescued by the Coast Guard. The gnarly stories are the ones where shyster coyotes swindle a group. They demand more money, abandon them to die, even murder them once they get their pay. Put them in leaky, overcrowded boats. Leave them in the trunks of cars on a hot day. Guide them into the desert and then disappear. And worse. But those are mostly stories from Europe or the U.S.-Mexico border. This is Canada. Nasty stuff like that doesn't happen here, does it?

Well, I could make sure it doesn't. I could help these boys. All I need to do is pick up my cellphone and call Officer Olsen. Hmm, *what* cellphone? Or sneak up to the bridge and use the radio. I have to get someone to chase after the guys who just robbed us, anyway.

Us? What am I thinking? I'm not part of this, and I should be looking after my own arse. I don't know how many of Arturo's injuries are from the robbers and how many from the captain, but there's sure no uncle-nephew thing going on there. And if the captain starts looking cross-eyed at me, I'm in way bigger doodoo than what skipping school today will cost me. No one even knows where I am! Not Mom or Dad, not Officer Olsen. Okay, I'm up for Dumb-Ass of the Decade. Totally deserve it.

Gregor, what should I do?

Dude, list the options.

I could hide. I could swim away. Or I could take my chances and pretend everything's cool.

Or?

Arturo stirs beside me, moans in his sleep. The red imprint of the captain's fist is on his cheek. I saw it being applied. He needs rescuing, I think. So do the boys. There are enough of us that we could mutiny. Lock the captain up so he can't pull anything. Then I could steer them all back to Horton Island. I'd be a hero. Officer Olsen would be proud of me. I just need to organize it.

Mutiny. Cool, bro.

I walk back up to the eating nook. Conversation freezes as I draw near. Everyone but Danillo is here.

"Hey guys," I say, looking at Pequeño, since he's the friendliest. "Want to come downstairs and make a plan?"

Pequeño looks at the others, then at the floor. Someone rolls his eyes. Someone coughs. The others glance toward the bridge, then stare at me, not in a friendly way.

"Come on. We're all in this together," I say, wishing I could shove the words back in my mouth as soon as they're out.

I turn and walk down to Arturo. To my surprise, the boys file after me, padding silently down the companionway. We arrange ourselves around Arturo's sleeping form.

"You think the captain's delivering you to somewhere nearby and everything's going to be cool, don't you?" I address them.

"Not anymore," Sebastian grumbles.

"Like he has told us," Gabriel says. "And like we'd tell you if we knew."

"What do you know?" Lucas challenges me with a tight face.

"I know how these operations work," I lie. "The coyote's always in it for himself."

They just glower.

"I know how to launch the dinghy. We could all get to shore and I'll get you help. Arturo, too," I add, watching the closed eyes and deep breathing of the first mate. "Help to stay in Canada," I add when no one says anything.

"Do you have a cellphone?" Gabriel asks.

"No."

"Do you have a gun?"

"No."

"Get Danillo down here," Sebastian orders Pequeño.

I give Pequeño a nervous nod.

The door bursts open a moment later. It's Danillo with the captain and Pequeño on his heels.

The captain's face is almost as smashed in as Arturo's, but it seems more puffed up from anger than swelling right now.

"Private conference, is it?" he snarls, eyes burning into me.

"*Conspirando para escapar*," comes Arturo's voice, startling me. Uh-oh. How long has he been awake and listening? I don't need his words translated to understand *conspiring to escape*. My gut tightens to a hard ball. Betrayed! And I was about to help rescue Arturo. Stop trusting any of them, I order myself too late.

"He thinks we're your prisoners, not paying customers," Sebastian says with a shaky chuckle. "Thinks *you're* the boss, not us."

"He thought Arturo might like to come, too," Lucas says with a laugh.

"Doesn't have a phone or gun, though," Sergio informs the captain. "So he says."

"You still letting him off at Nanaimo?" Danillo inserts, but without the ridiculing tone of the others.

Pequeño studies the floor and half hides behind Danillo.

"Arturo!" the captain snaps.

"Yes, Captain." Arturo sits up in bed, wavers for a moment like he's dizzy, then stands and waits. He's a pathetic sight, welts on his back and chest, his mashed face the colour of meat gone bad.

"Show Owen the engine room. Demonstrate how we keep a tight ship around here."

What does *that* mean?

"Danillo and the rest of you, help Arturo if he needs it. For your own good."

I feel arms grab mine. I'm half led, half dragged to the salon, where they open the hatch door to the engine room. Below me, squeezed in beside the mechanical works, is a very large, empty dog cage. Big enough to fit a St. Bernard or Great Dane.

. . .

ARTURO

Thinks he's as intelligent as a raven? Maybe he should compare himself to a dodo bird instead.

Anyway, he cooked his own goose. I wish I could have warned Owen, but what was the use? At least Captain is done being mad at me for now.

Owen reminds me of a baby-faced social worker named Jaime who used to risk his life to roam the streets of Guatemala City. A save-the-world type straight out of college, he wore carefully ripped jeans, expensive skateboard shoes, oiled hair, and an overconfident smile.

He thought he could rescue abandoned kids, tame gang leaders, and outwit crooked police with his smarts

and charm. But I knew he was different than other social workers the day he showed up by himself with a
hamper of bread and blankets.

"I'm celebrating one year on the beat," he said. We
had never met a social worker who'd lasted more than
two months.

"Don't need blankets," one of my kids insisted, arms
crossed, eyes narrowed.

"Yeah, you can't make us go to the shelters," said another.

"Of course I can't," he replied. "You think I don't
know that gang members force you to join up when you
sleep in the shelters? That's why you need blankets —
for sleeping outside, away from them."

My mouth gaped like the others.' "And you're not
telling the police where we are?" I challenged him.

"I trust them even less than you do," he stated, holding my eyes.

As the other kids took the blankets and bread and
moved away, he gestured for me to sit beside him. I did,
though I had the buzz that made me ready to leap up
and run at a second's notice.

"You're different," I finally said.

He smiled. "You're different, too. Like a dad to these
kids. Wish there were more like you. But ..." And then I
got the lecture about how some schooling would lead us
all to better things, and how a friend of his had started
a program to educate street kids.

I listened for a few minutes, then rose and sprinted
away. He didn't try to grab me. Didn't follow. The police didn't come looking for us that night.

So we let him hang with us sometimes after that. We took the food he offered. Soup, tortillas, bananas. He explained to me about breaking the chain of violence. It took a few months to convince me, but finally I decided to try the program he kept on about. With my group.

We were due to meet Jaime the morning the guards chased us to the dumpster. Sometimes I wonder if he's still working the streets of Guatemala City, pondering where I am. And I torture myself endlessly with the question of whether Freddy and the boys survived.

CHAPTER NINE

OWEN

Shouldn't have tried to be a hero, Gregor tells me.

"Why not? You told me to. And you were one."

Too little too late. And I'm a bad influence on you, remember?

I don't answer that. I don't want him here in the cage with me. I jump as the engine kicks up. Okay, we're off to somewhere. My ears are ringing and sweat pours from my armpits. Here in *Archimedes*'s innards, the reek of diesel invades my nostrils. The heat builds up and the yacht rocks as it negotiates its way through swells. Good thing I have a sailor's stomach.

My right side presses against the metal wires as I try to curl up in the cage. The question surging through my brain is what's going down next? I pull off my shirt and wrap it around my head to mute the engine's violence on my eardrums. The din quiets as the yacht settles down to cruising speed. Hours tick by, marked only by the occasional footfall above in the salon. My stomach gnaws, my throat feels like sawdust, I long to see or hear another human being. The thirst grows until I can hardly swallow.

Shuffle, shuffle. Am I sharing the engine room with a large rat? No, I spot Pequeño squirming toward me. I realize he's small enough to access this place from the chain locker through the tunnel-like space where the cables run. My heart leaps at seeing him.

"Here, I brought you water," he says, squeezing a small paper cup between the wires of the cage, spilling precious drops in the process.

"Thanks," I reply, trying not to pour it all down my gullet in one go.

"They'll give you food later."

"Good." Then, "How'd you get on this boat, Pequeño? Why do you want to move to Canada without your family?"

He offers a weak smile and looks around, as if expecting someone to be listening in. "We're the lucky ones."

I wait for him to go on.

"The *pandillas* in our country — the gangs. They make kids join them."

"Make them?"

He pulls himself up until he's sitting cross-legged beside my cage. He doesn't respond immediately.

"My older brother was in a gang once," I say to encourage him.

"My older brother, too," he says with a sigh. "Your brother still is?" he asks.

I shake my head.

"They kill him like mine?"

I bite my tongue, grip the sides of the cage. "No. He decided to get out."

Pequeño's eyebrows slant downward in disbelief. "In Guatemala, you don't decide anything. They decide if they want you. They shoot you if you don't join them. They shoot you if you want to leave after you join."

My throat goes thick. I reach fingers through the bars to touch the boy, who has buried his face in his hands. My fingers don't quite reach.

"Tell me about Guatemala," I say, fearful he'll leave.

"They come into the schools," he says. "Even private schools with guards. They came to ours. They held a gun to the principal's head. They visited each classroom, choosing the boys they wanted. They made the boys leave with them. No choice. Some teachers tried to hide us. Some teachers got shot for doing that."

"Can't the police stop them? What do parents do?"

"Gangs pay police. Parents cry." He hangs his head.

I hold my breath, trying to process the nightmare.

"How did you all get on this boat?" I ask in a gentler tone.

"We're the lucky ones," he repeats. "Our parents have money. Our parents got scared. They paid Captain to take us away. Lots of money." He studies his hands. "So I wouldn't end up like my brother. Dead for warning our school that they were coming again."

I wipe moisture from my face. "My brother did the same." I choke out the words. "Saved me."

"But they didn't kill him."

I pause, then shake my head slowly.

"Canada is a better country," Pequeño declares.

Our eyes lock. I'm struggling to keep mine dry.

Sunlight spills into the engine room. Someone has lifted the hatch door above us.

"What's this, a pity party?" Danillo's voice cuts through the space.

"Get away from him, little shit," he orders Pequeño. Pequeño scrambles back toward his hiding place.

"Hungry?" Danillo asks me.

I gaze at the bulging plastic bag in his hands. He drops down beside me and lifts something from the bag. He shoves a thin ham sandwich through the bars. Mustard oozes out in the process.

"Oops, the apple won't fit," he pronounces, and lifts it to his mouth to take a giant bite. The juice runs down his chin. He licks at it slowly, then wipes his face with his sleeve.

"Don't worry. We've all spent time in this cage. Except Pequeño."

"Why not Pequeño?"

"Captain would never admit it, but he has a little bit of a soft spot for Pequeño, given he's the youngest and smallest, I guess. Anyway, Captain calls it 'keeping a tight ship.'"

I say nothing, laying into the sandwich.

"Guess you got checkmated this game," Danillo continues. "You were only ever a pawn, anyway."

"And what does that make you?"

He laughs but ignores the question. "Arturo says you wanted an adventure. Says you don't have any friends except a Coast Guard officer. Are you some kind of spy? Because we don't like people who hang out with the Coast Guard."

"I'm a kid who lives on a small island. Everyone on the island knows the Coast Guard guy. Doesn't mean anything. I'm here 'cause I'm an idiot. Got on the wrong boat."

"Got that right," Danillo says. "But Captain says you'll be useful for helping to earn back some of the money stolen."

"Like how?" My stomach goes sour.

"Captain tells us stuff on a need-to-know basis. Evidently we don't need to know that yet."

He's in the process of sliding a cookie between the wires when the engine starts a coughing fit beside us. The cookie drops into the cage and breaks into pieces as the boat lurches.

"Uh-oh," Danillo says and leaps up to the salon like a jack-in-the-box. The hatch door slams shut. I get on my hands and knees to search for the cookie pieces even as my ears tune in to the engine losing power beside me.

"Fuel problem," I diagnose. "Not good."

• • •

ARTURO

Archimedes is well out into the Strait when the engine throws a punch. Its revs grow weaker as the rpm runs down. I am on duty; Captain has been moping over coffee in the salon for hours. The boys have scattered.

"*Mierda!*" Captain curses, bursting onto the bridge.

"I didn't do anything!" I protest in Spanish.

"Sounds like we're running out of fuel, but there's no way! We have plenty! Call Danillo to be lookout while we check it out."

"I'm here," Danillo says from behind, also in Spanish. "I'll watch the bridge."

"Good lad. We'll let *Archimedes* know there's no room for trouble today."

I follow Captain to the engine room, grabbing the tool box on the way. The big man and I drop down and squeeze past the cage like the island boy is not even there.

Captain checks the fuel and tinkers with the throttle cable. I check the air filter.

"I don't see a problem," Captain mumbles around a wrench in his mouth.

"Sounds like the throttle being pulled back," I say in Spanish, puzzled. "Should I restart the engine?"

"I don't know what you're saying, but you seem way too worried about the throttle cable," comes a voice in English from beside us. "Don't even think about restarting the engine, if that's what's on your mind, 'cause it's the engine fuel filter, not the throttle cable."

Captain turns and glares at the prisoner. Owen cocks one eyebrow back at him.

"Let me out and I'll fix it," the gringo offers.

"Nice try," Captain says, turning his back on the dog cage. He reverts to Spanish. "Arturo, the engine seems hot. Try the water pump."

With momentary relief that Captain still values my skills over Owen's, I take a screwdriver from the tool box, lie on my back, and wriggle under the raw water pump. I apply pressure gradually.

"Arrgh!" Captain shouts as dirty water squirts out the bleed screw spout and splashes us.

Mierda. I lift my soaked shirt away from my clammy skin.

"That's certainly working," Owen says.

If I were not under the engine, I would spit at the sarcastic island boy who keeps making me look bad.

But Captain has twirled around. "What makes you think you know what is wrong?" he demands in English.

"And what's in it for me to answer that?" *el estúpido* replies.

Captain raises the wrench in his hand. I hold my breath. Then he lowers it and grimaces.

"Arturo, boy, let the dog free," he mutters in Spanish.

I contemplate turning the cage upside down first, just to rattle him. Instead, I unlock it, swing the door open, and sweep my arms mockingly to show the prisoner the way out. I am not braced for the kick the Captain applies to my backside for the effort. A yelp escapes my lips. The buzz suggesting that I hit someone is almost overpowering.

"Back to the bridge," Captain orders.

I walk away, standing tall, after shooting poison-dart eyes at the stowaway/would-be engineer.

CHAPTER TEN

OWEN

The coffee gurgles its warm way down my throat. The captain makes it for me himself, leaving Arturo on watch.

"Not as useless as I thought," the captain says, referring to the twenty minutes it took to me to disassemble the engine fuel filter, clean it, reinstall it, and bleed the fuel system. "I'd offer you a first mate's position if I trusted you more than I can throw you, which I don't."

Am I supposed to say thanks to that? I seem to have inadvertently made an enemy of Arturo by proving handier than him. But I had to help. How am I supposed to escape if we're stuck mid-Strait? And I *am* good at boat maintenance and repair, especially when it comes to this model. Thanks mostly to my brother's patient coaching, back when he was a good guy.

So far, no one has ushered me back below decks. But neither are they leaving me alone long enough for me to approach the radio on the bridge or to leap overboard.

My parents have been at their conference for three days now and are surely wondering why I haven't phoned them or answered their calls. I've missed two days of school, enough for someone to raise an alarm. Maybe today Officer Olsen will decide it's more than hooky and put out some kind of missing report on me, if he hasn't already.

I cringe at the worry I must be causing my parents, who trusted me to be on my own. Dad will be trying to calm Mom, who will be thinking the worst, after what my brother put them through. I imagine them spending half their time in Miami talking by phone to Officer Olsen, the police, and my school, and making arrangements to abandon the conference and fly home. The fine residents of Horton Island will be combing the place for me, and boaters will be getting reports to keep on the lookout.

Have such reports reached the captain? It'll make him nervous, for sure. I'm causing a pack of trouble. Your fault, Gregor. You encouraged me.

Not my fault and you know it.

And here on board? The boys are acting like everything's normal, I guess. Danillo is creaming Lucas at chess, Pequeño is studying birds through binoculars while sprawled in a window seat. Gabriel — the one who likes baking, I'm told — is burning brownies in the oven, and the linebacker duo of Sebastian and Sergio have their heads hunched together over photos of their family.

The captain is studying nautical charts, pencilling stuff into a notebook, and glancing regularly at his expensive watch.

Over the next few hours, I get included in games of chess and Battleship, Pequeño loans me his skateboarding magazine (never mind that it's in Spanish), and others pepper me cautiously with more questions about Canada.

To keep my mind off the mess I've gotten myself into, I pretend for the moment that I really am on a cruise. It's way better than the boat trip to school, which lasts less than half an hour and typically features pissing rain and cold as raw as a polar bear's behind. There's hardly ever anyone on that water taxi between the ages of ten and forty-two (the driver's age) except me. And the school itself is as short of guys who pay me a second's notice as it is of good-looking girls.

Not like in Toronto, where I was ruler of the universe — for a while. Wanted for my talent for hotwiring boats, admired for being Gregor's kith and kin, I had it made at school and, after the bell rang, on the water. The Waterfront Gang ushered me in like I was a Hollywood star. We had fun for months until a certain dark and stormy night. The rest is lousy history. Including the abrupt move to Nowhere Land to separate me from the "bad influence" crowd. But we all miss Gregor. Does he miss us? I press my fist into my hurting heart.

You haven't made friends because you keep waiting for me to arrive and help you, brother. Stand up on your own two feet already. But remember to never, ever tell Mom and Dad —

Time to think of something else. My current situation on *Archimedes* may suck, but it's a situation. And I intend to stay sharp as a crab's pincer till I find a way out of it. No thanks to the other boys, who think this cruise is a snooze, or to the Artful Dodger, who I'm beginning to think is as dodgy as his pretend uncle from hell. Or is he just moody and back-and-forth on trusting me? Maybe hasn't experienced a lot of trust in his life. Maybe I should cut him some slack for that?

Screech! Screech! Screech!

"A bunch of seagulls," Pequeño says, appearing beside me.

I smile and look aft and up. "Bunch? No. The correct collective term for seagulls is *flock*."

"Whatever." He smiles.

"How about for eagles?" Gabriel points as two appear high in the sky, drawing neat figure eights.

"A convocation. And it's a murder of crows, a colony of vultures, and an unkindness of ravens."

"Is that true?" Lucas questions.

"That's silly," Pequeño says with a giggle.

"What's a boatload of boys?" the captain weighs in.

"Depends what they're up to," I joke. "But maybe all these birds mean we're near land?"

"Captain!" The shout comes from Arturo. The big man dashes to the bridge. His whistle blows, and in the melee that follows, I sprint to the stern deck and leap up into the dinghy. Not because I'm part of the hide-and-seek routine, but because that's where I hid my stuff last night and I'll need it for escaping. Was it only last night I was a free man innocently hitchhiking to Nanaimo? And now I'm leagues to the southwest.

• • •

ARTURO

It's nice to see land, even if it means the clients have to hide as a precaution. Normally, this would be my favourite part: dropping anchor, transferring the clients to the forested hideaway Captain calls the safe house, then waving goodbye and heading back south. That's when it's just Captain and me, with a thick wad of cash each: our well-earned salaries. There's some peace and quiet, and he lets me eat full meals. I intend to put my small but growing savings toward the day Captain dumps me, if he ever does. Happily, my crushing fear of being forced back to street life dwindles with each payday.

But the empty safe has changed things, including Captain's mood.

"Return Owen to the cage," Captain snaps. "He's hiding in the dinghy."

Hiding in the dinghy? Like that's going to do him any good. Like no one would notice and he could escape. I smile at the power I've just been handed. I can follow orders by recapturing the stowaway and stuffing him back into the dog cage. Or … I glance toward the pilothouse. What if, instead, I helped him lower the dinghy and escaped with him? Wouldn't that shock Captain? Ah, but then there would be the small matter of the bullet holes that would sink us once Captain fired on us. Not to mention the bullet holes in us. Oh well, stowaway, not today.

I sigh as I head toward the dinghy, hoping for the island boy's own sake that he co-operates, so Captain doesn't have to lend a nasty hand.

"You don't have to be his lackey," Owen says as I steer him to the cage, shut the door, and click the lock on him.

I have never heard the word before, but I can guess its meaning. "I am first mate," I spit back, straightening my shoulders. "He choose me. He train me. He pay me. He reward me one day. Am no lackey."

"He's cruel," Owen says, gripping the bars and leaning toward me. "You're not. He doesn't deserve you. You deserve better."

A bolt of warmth tears through my body and jolts my chest. For a moment, my heart glows with unchartered strength. Then it sputters like an ignition that turns over, but does not catch.

My eyes cloud until the sight of Owen in the dog cage in front of me becomes a vision of my shoeshine boys in the dumpster. They are pressed together, shivering, but bravely mute, as the guards' shouts draw near. Breathing in little gasps, trusting that I have saved them.

"The rest are in the Dumpster!" Heart-piercing screams. And Captain: "Good on you for keeping the street-kid population down."

Too many of them, because I wasn't cruel enough to turn them away.

My mind flicks farther back to my earliest memories. I am curled in a ball as the looming shadow of my stepfather applies his balled-up fists to my tiny body. This fades into memories of lashings from older street kids, one after another, and finally the belt of the captain.

If Owen thinks I have choices, it's because he's from a different world. A world I don't know or deserve.

And yet, one more memory thrusts itself on me: my hand rising over one of my misbehaving street kids. The veins in my forehead pulsing, a buzzing like from a power tool, the grit of teeth on teeth as an inner battle rages.

Thoughts of Jaime the social worker. And my promise to be the break in the chain.

The hand slowly lowering itself.

Not cruel. Deserve better. My chest threatens to burst open and spew out a lifetime of torment and longing. I stand tall and hold my breath to keep it locked inside.

"Captain just robbed," I finally blurt out. "He having hard time. He is my — he needs my — we need lock you up for safety, Owen. Yours and ours. Sorry."

Why did I say sorry? I turn and flee toward Captain, leaping two and even three steps at a time to put distance between Owen and me before he can reply. He is not my friend. I have no friends. I have never had friends.

• • •

For the next few hours, it is the usual routine. *Archimedes* hovers offshore until dark, water lapping at its hull, the scent of cedar trees coming from shore. Then it happens: the flash of light. A signal. Followed by the hiss of Captain's whistle and a tumble of boys out of cupboards.

"Get your sorry bodies and duffle bags into the dinghy, now!" barks Captain. "And Arturo, fetch the dog."

Owen says nothing as I swing open the cage door. He drags himself up to the salon, lifts his small bag to his chest, and files to the waiting dinghy beside the others with shoulders slumped, face fallen.

My heart races ahead of the oars I pull on as we glide across the black water toward the pulses of light. There is a soft thud as the bow nudges shore, and a large, hairy hand grabs the rope I toss.

"All yours, Stanton," Captain says as the boys stumble ashore.

The burly, scar-faced safe-house keeper, whose eyes I never dare meet, grunts and says, "Move it, vermin."

The boys shiver as they file to the tumbledown house with a roof that wears a thick coat of moss. They may suspect something is up, but so far it is all going according to plan. They are herded into the house's windowless basement by Stanton and his two gun-toting men.

Seated on the damp concrete floor, they get sandwiches and lukewarm coffee, which they down without complaint. Captain and I are waved toward rickety chairs placed in front of the stairs to bar the boys' escape. Stanton's men, smelling of sweat and cigarettes, serve the two of us doughnuts with our sandwiches and coffee. As I lick sugar crystals from my lips, I spot Danillo watching me. *Eat your hearts out, boys.*

Captain moves upstairs to talk with Stanton. I cringe when their raised voices drift down. "You just have to wait for a portion of your pay," Captain is saying.

Finally the two come down with the phone. I want to breathe easy now, because this is where each boy gets one phone call to tell his parents or guardians that he has arrived safely. The parents in turn deliver the second half of the money to Captain's Guatemala contact, who notifies Captain of receipt. Then the boys are released. Neat, organized, and fair.

But there is a hitch this time, and I do not like it.

"Boys," Captain says, addressing the group with his deep voice in Spanish. "Because we lost so much money to the pirates that we can't pay our kind hosts here, you each have a choice. When you call your parents to let them know you've arrived, you must request that they double the balance of money they are due to deposit —"

"What? No way!" some of the boys interrupt.

"As I was saying," Captain resumes in a booming voice that makes the boys shrink back, "they must double the second half of the payment, in which case we will promptly release you, or you will be held in a nearby labour camp until you work off the extra money required."

Not the work camp again. I sigh. It has been a while since Captain pulled this. But I know this routine as well as I know the usual one.

I scan their faces. Mouths ajar, eyes narrowed, arms crossed, bodies slumped in resignation. There is mumbling, there are a couple of protests, and one or two tears. And then there is Owen, who merely looks confused, since he does not understand Spanish. Captain does not leave the gringo in the dark for long. He switches to English.

"I will now pass the phone around. No funny business; we're standing by listening and can cut you off. Everyone gets one call. Everyone except Owen, whom I've already volunteered for labour camp."

I smile. That will teach Owen to stow away, play first mate with his mechanical skills, and get too friendly with the clients. But the moment that thought registers, I frown and lower my head. He has never done me any harm, and so what if he showed me up once on boat mechanics? The guy stumbled into our operation innocently. He doesn't deserve what Captain's about to dish out. No one does. "Owen will do so alongside Arturo," Captain carries on as my jaw loosens and my chest clamps up, "who I know will set a great example with how hard he works. In other words, Arturo, you'll be joining the labour operation for however many weeks it takes."

What? Never before has Captain forced me into the work camp. *Never!* How dare he — I leap up, tingling at full buzz. But before I can say a word, Captain's big hand comes down firmly on my back and steers me to the circle of distressed boys, then presses on my shoulders until I sit down on the butt-chilling concrete.

I consider leaping up and shouting at him, arguing, refusing to go. But one glance at Stanton and I know it's just what he's waiting for.

I try to reason it out: Captain is pissed off about Owen sneaking on board and about the pirate incident. My boss's anger is irrational; he's taking it out on me.

He'll be more reasonable in the morning. I can let my defiance loose then. Timing is everything, I've learned in my three years with him. But whatever happens, he'll be paying for this. In burnt meals or worse. I squint my eyes and give him a look as my fists ball up of their own accord.

CHAPTER ELEVEN

OWEN

A five-star hotel this is not. We're handed a ratty blanket each, which we wrap around ourselves on the concrete floor. Pequeño sleeps between Danillo and Arturo, the first mate unable to hide a grim face ever since the captain left him with us. I'm on the outside of the circle. Like I always have been, I remind myself.

"Coffee. Rise and shine, kids."

I prop open an eye as my nose determines that hot coffee is indeed in the room.

"Get up, now!" The goons' voices drop any pretence of cheer.

"Must be morning," Gabriel mutters.

I sit up fast as a coffee cup appears beside me. Ignoring the ripe scent of unwashed bodies, I sip it like I'm at the bakery cafe back on Horton Island.

We've barely finished our coffee when the guards jerk their heads toward the stairs.

"Up and out. Get a move on." One points his gun to emphasize the order.

As we file past a small table near the stairs, I snatch a folded-up newspaper and stick it under my shirt. A dude's got to keep up on what's happening in the world while on extended vacation.

"Hey!" Lucas's voice. Outside, the goons are pushing him apart from the rest of us. "Bye, guys. Text me when you can, okay?" he shouts as he's shoved into a car.

"He's free," Danillo states with a grim face. "His parents paid up."

"I wonder," I say. All that's clear is that we aren't. I see no opportunity to bolt before we're directed into the back of a rusty unmarked white van dimly lit by small holes in the walls and floor. No seats, of course. Just before the back doors slam shut, I look out at the water. No sign of *Archimedes* in the early morning mist.

Arturo sits apart from the others. I should feel sorry for him, but lack the energy for it.

"Sorry about your demotion," Danillo baits the first mate as the engine roars and our ride jerks ahead. "But it's only for a few days. Then your captain will come save you and put you back on the high seas to fleece more clients."

"Stop being mean to Arturo," Pequeño speaks up bravely.

"Or what?" Danillo flings back.

"Thought you'd be released," I say to Danillo, "given your parents own a yacht."

"*Owned* a yacht," he says in a pinched voice. "Sold it to put me on *Archimedes*."

"And you thought if you just showed up here," I say, "no one would arrest you or send you back? You'd find a new school to go to, send for your parents, and live happily ever after?"

He hesitates. "Yes. That's why our families sent us. Kids get a special break. Amnesty. They're allowed in with hardly any questions, no punishment. They never get sent back."

I shake my head. "That's what the captain told your parents? And they believed it?"

Everyone's staring at me except Arturo. The boys' faces have gone pale. Arturo turns toward the rusty wall as if he needs to study it. He and the captain have done this many times; he must know that when the boys are turned over to authorities, they don't always get to stay, nor manage to bring their parents in.

"Sorry, guys, but it's not that easy," I say. "The captain just wanted his money, so he said whatever your parents wanted to hear. If you're caught you'll be detained and maybe deported. Held until an immigration hearing, then —"

"But we won't end up in prison or beaten?" Sebastian asks.

"No," I reply, trying to think what else I've heard from Officer Olsen.

"Then it's okay," Sergio says. "Better than Guatemala."

"And we *might* get to stay," Gabriel adds with a smile.

It's my turn to stare at my schoolboy companions, who seem altogether too relaxed. Then, for an instant, my eyes meet the first mate's.

"Arturo, you're a different matter," I inform him.

The van takes a tight corner and we're hurled against each other. My head bangs against the side of the van. My upper body lands in Arturo's lap. He says nothing, just pushes me away.

"If you're caught, you'll get arrested and put in a youth detention centre for a while. But given your age, you have a chance of eventually being allowed to stay. It's the captain who'd get his boat seized and sold. And he'd get major prison time."

Silence.

I pull out the newspaper crumpled inside my shirt and tug my headlamp out of my pack.

"Where'd you get a newspaper?" Danillo asks.

"It was in the basement."

"Catching up on your stock reports?" he sneers.

"Shit!" I say.

"What?" several voices ask, leaning toward me.

"Gulf Island Teen Boy Goes Missing," I read the headline, heart sinking. "Search and Rescue is looking for me. My poor parents ..."

"Like anyone's going to come looking for you here," Sebastian mumbles.

"Did you tell anyone you were leaving?" Gabriel asks.

"Did anyone see you go?" Sergio adds.

"Or do they think you've run away or drowned?" Danillo inserts.

I take a deep breath, overwhelmed with guilt, too miserable about what I'm putting my parents through to answer.

I'm so sunk into myself that I'm barely aware of our vehicle as it lurches along a dirt road we glimpse only through a dinner-plate-sized, rusted-out hole in the floor. Soon enough, it gets used as a toilet, and later as a place to puke through.

"Oh man," objects Sebastian, holding his nose.

It's well after dark when the van jerks to a halt. Flashlights blinding us, we're led over a soft carpet of pine needles through sweet-smelling forest to a shipping container, a rectangular steel box the size of a train car. We stand just inside the body-odour-infused space, holding our packs and the thin blankets given us at the safe house, gazing at a row of filthy foam mattresses, when the doors slam shut behind us and what sounds like a steel bar drops into place.

It's pitch black until I fish out my headlamp.

"We're hungry!" Sebastian shouts at the locked doors. "We need food."

"And water," Gabriel adds.

"And you have to let us out for the toilet," comes Pequeño's voice.

"Shh, Pequeño," Arturo says quietly. "There is bucket for that; I find for you. Try to sleep. Here by me."

A ripple of laughter outside, the crunch of boots walking away, then silence.

• • •

The screech of the bar lifting wakes us at dawn. Our throats parched, stomachs rumbling, still shivering from the night's cold, we're ushered out. I scratch the itchy red bedbug bites that cover my body.

A bearded guard wearing a gun in a holster points to the creek beside us. "Drink there."

Some of the boys hesitate. "Water's clean," snaps the second armed guard, whose greasy, shoulder-length hair is crowned by a bald spot. Baldie, I name him.

I know better than to take the chance. As the others walk over and kneel beside the stream, I dash back into the shipping container to grab my water purification tablets. My hands close over the bottle before Baldie's fingers close around the back of my neck and he hauls me out again. I fill my water bottle from the stream and pop in a tablet. I wish I had enough for everyone, but I don't.

Arturo's and my eyes meet. He resembles a cowed dog, tail between his legs, miserable but obedient. He has said little since we arrived and doesn't look in the mood for communicating now, either. I wonder if this work camp thing happens all the time. Maybe, but from the way he reacted last night, I suspect he's not usually forced to be part of it.

Our "camp" site is a mess. Piles of wood slash and garbage surround our unventilated shelter. Nearby, the two guards' small trailer has a tarp strung up beside it, under which a picnic table, ice chests, propane barbecue grill, and more garbage lie. Beyond that are two other garage-sized shipping containers. One has a steel bar securing it, like ours.

Our bearded guard approaches the locked container, lifts the bar, opens the doors, and starts shouting.

More than a dozen sleepy-looking men file out, all in their early twenties. They're in torn-up undershirts and trousers, and they're as skinny and dark-skinned as the people on posters for starving people in Africa. They stare at us, then walk to the river to drink and wash like it's a long-established routine. I catch some French words. French Africans, I decide. The other container, doors open, is filled with shovels, heavy-duty vinyl bags, and trays of seedling trees in paper cones.

Tree-planting camp. I've got cousins who've had summer jobs planting trees for forestry companies in back-of-beyond northern places. It's hard work, but good money. They lived in tents, got fed really well, and gathered each evening around a campfire for guitar playing and singing.

This feels more like a prison camp, perhaps one specializing in illegal immigrants. *And no one knows where we are.* Five days since my parents took off. Three days since I stowed away. And the search for me is on.

"Line up!" the bearded guard barks.

Within thirty minutes, we're outfitted with boots, gloves, and tree-seedling bags, which hang around us on suspenders like mailbags.

I smother a smile as I glance at Arturo and Pequeño. Being the smallest of the bunch, they're wearing oversized boots and gloves with limp fingertips that hang halfway to the ground. Like small kids playing dress-up in adult clothes.

The men from Africa, who, like us, are handed bowls of porridge for breakfast, spoon the food into their mouths while watching us as if bemused at the arrival of novices.

After we eat, we're handed shovels and trained to aim them at the dirt in front of us, form a neat hole, bend at the waist to plant a small tree from our packs, then stand up and kick the hole shut with our boot heels.

"If you don't close the hole up all the way, we'll make you do it over," Beard informs us. "If you smush the seedling so the lower part is curved, you do it over *and* get an extra hour's work. And if you plant it too deep or too shallow, same thing."

Got it. Doesn't sound too hard.

"*Mierda*," Arturo mumbles under his breath.

"Fill your bags with seedlings," Baldie orders, jabbing his thumb at the trays. "Plant eight hundred or more a day and you get extra supper. When you run out of seedlings, walk back to the vehicle for more."

Arturo narrows his eyes and looks to the horizon, like he's thinking of running.

"Not fair —" Gabriel starts to protest, but Beard pushes him along with the rest of us into the white van half filled already with stacks of trays. The African team piles into a Jeep behind us, Baldie in the driver's seat. Doors slam shut and we're off, I assume to the tree-planting site. Pequeño leans into me as if seeking comfort.

"We'll be okay," I reassure him. "We'll work hard and get out of here." Or I'll find a way to disappear.

• • •

We plunge our shovels into the dirt, bend, and plant all day. The wind bites, the sun burns, the rough terrain trips us as often as possible. Hornets take turns with mosquitoes torturing us; soon our faces and ears are puffed up with bites and stings. Our boots rub till our feet are bleeding. We're each given a stale bun with a microscopic slice of cheese for lunch. None of us comes near planting eight hundred trees.

Our sharp-eyed guards keep us and the African team well apart while leaving no one a chance to disappear into the brush. Unlike our African neighbours, most of us are ordered to redo about a third of what we've planted.

"Hey-ho!" We look up. It's the French Africans packed into the Jeep, waving merrily at us as they head back to camp and we start our extra hour.

"*Bastardos*," Arturo mumbles.

"They probably did lots of extra time when they started," I try to reason.

"Yeah, we'll be rubbing it in when the next group of slaves arrives. If we're lucky enough to graduate," Sergio says bitterly.

"Cheer up. We're building muscles, experiencing the great Canadian outdoors, and adding to our resumés," I say.

"Shut up, freak," Sebastian replies.

And that's the end of that conversation.

At dusk, the van delivers us back to camp and an over-salty, thin chicken soup. Then we fall onto our mattresses, asleep before the first bedbug bite.

• • •

ARTURO

The second night, squeezed up against the far wall of the steel container, I find it hard to breathe. The place reeks of mould, damp, unwashed bodies, creek-washed clothes strung above us, and human shit.

"If only we had more air in here," mumbles Danillo.

"Doesn't help that the stupid bucket is so close," Gabriel complains, switching on his headlamp.

He means our night toilet.

I lift my fingers and run them down the wall beside me, shivering as they come away wet with condensation. Something uneven on the wall makes me sit up and reach for my headlamp. I feel six pairs of eyes watching in the dim glow as I identify two circles, each the size of a fist, several feet apart on the back wall and only a foot above the floor. They are covered by circular plates screwed on tightly.

"For hoses?" I mumble in Spanish, and the boys are soon pressed around me. "Anyone have a screwdriver?"

"Yeah, right."

"Breathing holes," I announce, still in Spanish, and whip out my pocketknife.

"Do they know you have a knife?" Pequeño asks in a small voice.

"Of course not," I warn.

Headlamp trained on the circles, knife blade applied to a screwhead, I work slowly, sweat running down my face, to oust the screws and free the plates.

"*Ventilación*," I say with satisfaction as I finish and hide the screws and circles of metal beneath my mattress. The boys take turns putting their mouths up to the holes and breathing deeply like they are nicotine addicts having a smoke.

"Can we expand them into escape holes?" Danillo asks in Spanish.

"We wish," Owen responds, obviously guessing the meaning of the Spanish word *escapada*.

It doesn't make a huge difference to the airflow, but it puts smiles on the boys' faces before they bed down again. I decide to screw the covers in place again, loosely, each morning.

. . .

Next day, I plant seven hundred seedlings, the second highest after Owen's 760. For a split second, I am proud. Then I realize it is not enough to "win" extra supper.

Pequeño plants the least because he has diarrhea from the creek, even worse than some of the other boys. The creek water may not be pure enough for the delicate systems of private-school boys, but if the students do not keep drinking water, they will soon collapse from thirst, I figure.

"Drink from my bottle. I am not sick," I urge

Pequeño, and I plant a few of my seedlings on the boy's assigned strip of land.

"Away from him!" Beard shouts.

I hustle back to my planting section.

Twice on the planting hill, when no one is looking, I pull out the cellphone I lifted from Owen's house that first night and dial Captain. I want to ask him how long we have to be here. But no surprise: we're in a dead spot. No reception.

"*Pineros!*" Baldie mocks us, using the Spanish word for illegal tree planters and waving his pistol. "Fancy-boy Latrinos. More trees, faster, if you want more food. No pampered children here. You complain like old women and take twice as long as our last truck-load of wetback trash."

I notice that the guards always lump Owen in with the schoolboys, never acknowledging that he's not Hispanic.

I double my efforts, but get it even worse than the others.

"Hey darkie," Beard taunts me. "Not Captain's pet anymore, eh? But so lucky to be planting trees with us. Way better than shining shoes. Hey, precious school-boys, does dark boy shine your shoes every morning before we open the doors? Har har!"

So funny. *Har har*, I think.

"Leave him alone," the twins say, standing together with their hands on their hips and directing fierce looks at the guards. It means a lot to me, even if Baldie and Beard just laugh.

Waving their pistols around, the men throw insults at the African team, too.

"Idiot gorillas, stop dragging your feet! Plant faster, or no supper!"

Worse than taunts, of course, the guards find more fault with my planting than with anyone else's, only as an excuse to lower my numbers and assign me extra time. It washes right off me; I have heard it all my life, and worse.

Ignore them and keep planting. Show the boys, who have less experience with this crap, how to handle it. Just like I did with my shoeshine boys. Don't reveal the slightest reaction. Be patient, practice self-control. The guards will get their own, eventually.

What doesn't wash off me is the thought that I shouldn't be here. My bitterness toward Captain is welling up like a blister in danger of popping. Where is he, anyway? All the other times Captain sent clients to the work camp, he and I relaxed on board *Archimedes*, waiting for them to finish. Then we split the money we got from the extra labour, which the clients were forced to do on some made-up excuse.

But why did Captain send me this time? Why should *I* be here sticking trees into stony ground, stumbling up and down rises littered with dead branches, stumps, and roots, and earning scratches and sores that bleed or swell purple? Did the robbery really put us so short that he needed my labour as well to cover the debt? That must be the reason. How long will it take to finish here, get rid of the boys, and head home with Captain? I can't help but wonder whether it is out of bad habit that I am still loyal to him.

The schoolboys complain of their hunger and thirst, and the racial slurs. They have no idea what any of those really are.

I notice that Owen, on the other hand, appears deaf to the jabs and does not utter a word of complaint. And, like me, he occasionally sneaks over to plant in Pequeño's section to keep the increasingly sick youngest boy from being assigned extra time for "laziness." How long before Pequeño drops? I worry. He reminds me of one of the youngest of my shoeshine squad. A little fragile, but always trying his hardest, setting an example.

• • •

By the fourth morning, I'm frantically concerned about Pequeño.

"Get up!" the guards shout from beyond the door as they lift the bar. I extend my hand to Pequeño, but he can barely struggle to his feet. When I let go, he drops back down to his sleeping bag and closes his eyes.

I lean down and hold my hand to his forehead. Sweat dampens my palm.

"Look at me, Pequeño," I say as the guards start kicking anyone who's not heading out the door. His eyelids flutter open, but his pupils seem glazed. I place my hand on his chest, then lower my ear to it. A sort of shuddering sound comes with each laboured breath.

"Out, you two!" Beard shouts, waving his gun.

"I come, but this one too sick to move. Needs doctor," I dare to say.

"He's just faking it to get out of work," Beard retorts. "We've seen it before. Get to work. I'll deal with the lazy one."

His shove gives me no choice. But I'm relieved when I see Beard emerge without Pequeño, then stroll back into the shipping container with some food and a water bottle.

"Where's Pequeño?" Owen asks as we climb into the van.

"They give him day off," I say hopefully. "Maybe are calling doctor."

. . .

One hour into planting, I form the opinion that Owen is a born tree-planting machine; the boy pauses only to sip water and call out words of encouragement to the others. Nor does the water ever make him ill. The gringo even offers advice to me once: "If the ground is soft, use your hands to close the hole. If it's hard, use your boot."

"Okay," I reply after some hesitation, and work hard to imitate my island friend.

That night, everyone is given a potato, a slice of ham, and an orange. Owen and I win large bowls of steaming chilli besides. Wordlessly, we share the chilli around the group evenly.

CHAPTER TWELVE

OWEN

Using a sharp twig to scratch on a patch of dried mud beside my foamie, I calculate that we've been tree planting for five days now. It has been over a week since I left home. My parents are definitely back by now, totally stressed out about my disappearing act, and without one clue to go on. Why didn't I at least leave a note?

Good thing they can't see what shape I'm in. My hands and feet are as calloused as bark, and I smell so putrid that the mosquitoes have almost given up tackling my torn-up skin. My stomach is shrunken, but my muscles are taut. I feel immune to devil's club, stinging nettles, hunger pains, torrential rain, and the guards' taunts.

Mind over matter. Survive. Unlike the other boys, I haven't fallen victim to diarrhea or fever. Only Arturo and I have ducked that fate so far. Nor has either of us picked up the deep, hacking cough that the twins have.

I'm no doctor, but it sounds like pneumonia. And now Gabriel is starting to cough.

"They need medical help," I tell the guards. "You need to get them out of here."

"They're fine," Baldie retorts.

"Give them more food and breaks if you want them to plant lots of trees for you," I press.

"What do you think this is, a vacation camp?" Beard snaps. "Shut up unless you want a bullet through your foot, like one of the gorillas got for trying to escape yesterday."

He's not lying. I heard the shot and the screams.

I turn and lope back to my tree planting, discouraged. And yet, as I look around, I remind myself I've got it way better than the others.

I have jeans, a fleece, and a parka, while the boys' school uniforms, which look ridiculous out here, have been torn to shreds by now and offer little protection from the cold, wind, and rain. I even have my wetsuit to pull on if I'm cold at night, and my rain poncho to protect me during the day.

Meanwhile, the twins, with their large frames, are suffering more than the rest of us from the starvation rations.

"Arturo, you okay?" I call out as he trips over some brush.

"Am okay," he says with a sheepish grin. "Gabriel," he calls to his left. "Is eagle watching us from sky. Smile!"

The guy never complains, I've noticed, and is always trying to cheer up the rest of the gang, despite how they used to order him around on *Archimedes*.

Like Arturo, I'm still healthy and a strong worker, I remind myself. And I have a goal: earning extra food for the others and trying to care for them at night.

Even so, I'm weakening by the day.

I wince to think what kind of panic I've caused my parents. Officer Olsen probably has a full-on manhunt going for me, but there's no way any kind of search is going to locate us here. Nor have our keepers indicated we'll be released anytime soon. *We have to escape.* Preferably before Pequeño, who is now so ill from a stomach bug that the guards leave him locked up all day in the shipping container, dies. Would Arturo be into escaping?

• • •

The next day, the monotony is broken by Danillo's shout. "Gabriel!" I look to where Gabriel was planting trees seconds ago. The other boys charge through the brush to where his limp form lies on the ground.

"Fainted," Sebastian rules.

Gabriel: always the skinniest.

"Hey! Back to work!" the guards shout, rushing toward the stalled tree-planters.

This is my chance. I drop behind a log, then roll down the hill, spiky grass and sticks pressing into me. When I reach the creek, I scramble up and splash through it, crouched down. Then I slip into dense forest and take off at high speed, zigzagging a little just in case one of the guards has a gun trained on me. When I spot a hole under a stump large enough to hide me, I dive in.

Burrowed in as far as possible, curled up like a frightened fox, I breathe in the moist smell of dirt. It's quiet here, otherworldly with veins of roots, almost cozy. No wonder groundhogs hang out underground till spring. Then I hear twigs crackling above. Boots moving. Boots pausing. I hold my breath. I can actually see a soiled red lace that has come undone on Beard's worn boot. I know it's Beard because Baldie has yellow laces and new boots. I could lift my fingers and tie those red laces for him if I wanted to. Or tie his two boots together.

He's that close, but so is the promise of freedom. Seconds tick by like hours. I breathe out again when the boots move on. There are miles of rough terrain here and thousands of stumps with holes under them. Besides, I figure he has to return to help Baldie stop the others from following my example.

• • •

It's nightfall when I guess they've given up. Yes! I can flee now, west toward the ocean, whose direction I've identified by the position of the sun and an occasional salt-tinged breeze. Maybe I can build a fire there till someone spots me. I know we're on the Strait of Georgia somewhere northwest of Texada Island, perhaps even as far north as Stuart Island. Remote but not entirely without logging roads or cabins. What wouldn't I give for a GPS to figure out my location right now, or a radio to contact someone with. Or my cellphone to call my parents.

Heart knocking against my rib cage, I crawl out of my hole and breathe in the tang of evergreen. Then I dig into my pockets for the two tools I've hidden on me for days in case this moment came: my compass and my headlamp.

Though I try to walk lightly, every footfall sounds to me like some jerk chomping on popcorn in a movie theatre. And I get less than a mile before my boots halt.

Nope, keep going, little brother. You're thinking about going back and releasing them. Dumb idea.

"Shut up, Gregor."

Last time you tried to help them, you got put in a dog cage, remember? Maybe they don't want to be broken out. And then there's Arturo. Who knows whose side he's on? You can always call the Coast Guard when you finally get somewhere.

"By then, more of them will have collapsed and some might have died. You know it. And Arturo's as fed up as the rest of us."

Or not.

I scoop up rocks and throw them through the air. Gregor shuts up. I kick the dirt one way, then the other. Eventually, my boots turn around.

I approach camp cautiously and wait at a good distance till the men have finished off a couple of beers. Beard tumbles into their trailer for the night. Baldie stays up, I'm guessing to catch me if I dare to sneak back. But he's soon asleep, slumped in his camping chair beneath an insect-swarmed lantern.

In slow mo, I slip up to our shipping container. With excruciating patience, I lift the bar slowly so that it doesn't make a sound. One by one, I tap the sleeping boys.

"File out barefoot," I whisper in their ears. "Carry your shoes and duffle bags." I grab my own pack.

Arturo stands, but doesn't move. Will he shout and wake the guards? Betray us? I shiver as I face him down. "Pequeño will die if we don't leave now," I say in a hushed tone.

Without a word, he leans down, sweeps Pequeño into his arms, and carries him out. Sergio leans on his brother Sebastian, both of them restraining their coughs; Danillo leads Gabriel.

I head toward the Africans' container to lift the bar, only to feel a knifepoint prick the back of my neck.

"Leave them," Arturo orders. "Not our *problema*."

Reluctantly, I back up. Then, like a night scout, I lead the boys away, sweat pouring down my back. As I pause on the hill above camp to let them put on their footgear, Arturo says, "No good."

"Huh?"

"They find us. I have idea."

"What kind of idea?"

He explains. I hesitate. Do I trust him?

Don't, urges Gregor.

I motion Danillo over and explain what we're up to. He gives me a thumbs-up and leads the group into a dense patch of trees to wait as Arturo and I creep back down the hill.

• • •

ARTURO

"Plan is we confuse guards," I elaborate to the island boy.

"Right," my companion replies with a twitchy smile.

We enter the container, push the mattresses to the rear, and arrange them to make it look like there might be a pile of boys under them. I remove the circles of metal on our ventilation holes.

Then, after closing the big doors and lowering the bar without a sound, we glance toward the still-sleeping guard under the tarp shelter and move through the grass to the rear of the container. Here we're out of sight of the trailer unless we peer around the corner to look.

"Ready?" I whisper, my heart going a gazillion beats per second, the electrical buzz powering up.

"Ready."

We squat, lean forward and scream into the ventilation holes till our shrieks are bouncing off the inside walls of the container.

"What the —" comes a growl from across the clearing.

I peek to see that Baldie is up and gripping his pistol, then banging on the little trailer's door to wake his partner.

Soon two groggy armed guards stumble over to the doors of the container, at the opposite end of where we're lurking.

"Shut up in there, y'hear?"

"Or we'll give you something to make a ruckus about!"

We wail and howl through our holes on the other

end even more dramatically. When I pause for breath, I'm grinning like a monkey.

The guards pound, shout, and finally lift the bar.

"Heeelp!" screeches Owen with all his strength as I move away. "Heeeelp!"

"Silence!" It's Beard, moving cautiously inside the container toward the mattresses, his pistol raised.

"Cover me," he orders his mate, who's standing just outside the doors, oblivious to me sneaking up behind them.

"Ugghh!" his mate says as I kick him in the butt hard enough to send him sprawling into the container. And before either of the men can leap back to the entrance, I clang the doors shut and put the bar down. I could light up a Christmas tree with the electricity dancing off me.

"Hey!" come echoey shouts from inside the container.

But Owen and I are too busy sprinting across the clearing to hear any more. First we lift chicken drumsticks off the guards' barbecue grill, then enter the smelly little trailer to collect more food, stuffing some into our mouths and the rest into the pockets of a tree-planting bag Owen throws on.

Grease coating my lips, I'm all but twirling with happiness at capturing the bastards and getting some food into me.

Then, *crack*!

I freeze and catch Owen's shoulder, almost choking on a mouthful.

Crack, crack, crack!

"They're trying to shoot their way out."

I nod grimly.

We dash up the hill and hustle our companions down to the van. Owen jumps into the driver's seat and reaches for the ignition.

"No keys!" he shouts.

"I'll check their trailer," Danillo says and dashes off, ducking to avoid any stray shots spitting out of the container.

"Or they've got the keys on them," Gabriel mumbles.

"No worries. I'll hotwire this thing," Owen rules.

"I help," I offer, leaping out after him.

"Hurry!" Sebastian urges. "Before they break out!"

Danillo returns empty-handed, but brightens when he sees Owen's and my heads under the hood.

We high-five one another as the van kicks into action. Then we dive into the front seat and keep our heads down as we roar away from the gunfire and whatever satellite phone the trapped men might be using. I picture the trail of dust we leave settling over the detested site.

CHAPTER THIRTEEN

OWEN

I manage to drive for an hour in the inky night until I spot a turnoff with a sign reading *Raven's Retreat*.

"A cabin. Maybe people and a phone," I say, veering the van up the rutted road.

The outline of a rustic cabin with neither lights nor vehicle in the driveway comes into view as the moon moves out from behind a cloud and dances on ocean waves below.

"Yes!" I shout. Never have I been so pleased to see the Georgia Strait.

We hop out and open the van's rear doors to release the others. Soon we're at the cabin's front door, where Arturo manages to pick the lock.

• • •

"That was way too close," Danillo says as we recount the details of our getaway while settled on a musty sofa in front of the crackling fireplace. "Lucky you guys knew how to jump-start the van."

"Not luck — skill," Sebastian rules.

I smile, but Danillo is certainly right that our escape was dodgy.

"I hope their bullets ricocheted off the walls of that container and into them," Gabriel says soberly.

"Don't say that," Pequeño says in a quiet voice.

"They probably had a satellite phone on them, even if the shooting didn't get them out," Sergio says.

"What I want to know is why you two stole a tree-planting bag," Danillo addresses Arturo and me. "Needed a souvenir?"

I smile as I position it in front of the fire.

"Food," Arturo explains proudly.

Everyone rushes forward and pushes hands into the bag's pockets.

"Share!" I order, and everyone steps back.

"Thanks, Owen and Arturo," Danillo says soberly as the others murmur their appreciation.

Holding some food in reserve for whatever future travels await, I help Arturo and Danillo distribute the cold, cooked chicken drumsticks.

The meat off my drumstick slides down my throat nicer than a corner store Slurpee on a summer's day.

"And a corncob!" Arturo announces, dangling it over Pequeño's glittering eyes. "All yours."

There's silence as we watch our pale friend chew on it, mumbling "thanks" as he licks his fingers.

Arturo rises and rifles through the cupboards. "Instant

coffee, cake mix, four cans of spaghetti, and rat poison."

Gabriel leaps up. "Spaghetti for breakfast. I'll make the cake now."

"Hold the rat-poison icing," Sebastian deadpans before breaking into a coughing fit.

Danillo checks the medicine cabinet. "Sleeping pills, aspirin, cough syrup, and a thermometer," he says, bringing the aspirin and thermometer to shivering Pequeño and the cough syrup to the twins and Gabriel.

"And blankets in this cupboard," Sebastian announces. A whiff of mothballs trails him back to the sofa.

We wrap Pequeño in a blanket, coax him to drink some water with the aspirin, and lift him into the nearest bedroom.

"Sleep till first light," I urge everyone, and most of the boys pad off to the bedrooms without argument.

I find pen and paper and write a note to the cabin owners explaining our emergency situation and leaving my home phone number with an offer to pay for everything.

Danillo, thermometer in hand, lowers himself into a chair beside Pequeño's bed. "I'll keep an eye on him tonight," he volunteers.

"Great. I'm going down to the shore to see if there's a boat."

"Good idea," Arturo says with a yawn.

Outside with my headlamp, I listen to the familiar sound of crickets and creaking tree branches; I even hear the crunch of deer hooves moving away. It feels like I'm back on Horton Island, a strangely exuberant notion. I count seventy-seven rickety stairs to the beach. There, I tremble with excitement as I spot a derelict boathouse. Any chance?

The upper hinge of the unlocked door almost falls off as I push it open. A good-sized vessel sits under a ragged tarp. I snatch off the cover and catch my breath. A very mildewed twenty-five-foot-long tugboat bumps gently against the piling. I rub dirt off where the name is painted: *Homeward Bound*.

Time to leap aboard and pretend it has just arrived at Steward Marina for a tune-up. Crawling hurriedly to the engine access cover, I lift it and find my heart beating ever more rapidly. A 135-horse Perkins diesel. Probably capable of twelve knots. Interior not in bad condition. Motorized dinghy on the back almost new. This tug's worth maybe $50,000 on the black market.

Stop. You're not stealing it or selling it or hot-wiring it for the Ontario gang. That's all over and done with. You're borrowing it to get people to medical help, and to get back to civilization. Time to go home. *Homeward Bound* will need some overnight repairs but —

"Nice," Arturo says from the doorway, startling me.

"Needs work, but I think it can take seven boys across the Strait."

"Awesome big time. Need help?"

"Wouldn't mind. Could have it ready to go by morning," I say hopefully.

"I your first mate," Arturo replies with a grin, reaching for a tool box and a generator on a dusty shelf of the boathouse. After a few tries, we get the generator going and turn off our headlamps to work under a pair of pull-cord hanging bulbs.

We work as efficiently as doctors in surgery, me on my back with my head between the engine and tool box, him handing me tools and offering suggestions.

"How about you test the batteries while I look at the fuel system?" I suggest.

"*No hay problema.*" And a minute later, "Dead."

"Hmm, hook up the battery charger and maybe we can start the old Perkins by morning."

"Okay."

"Half tanks. Not bad. I'm going to free up the throttle."

"Good idea," my first mate agrees.

"Damn. Cable's jammed and fuel system has some water in it."

"We empty water from fuel filter and hope," Arturo says.

And so it goes for hours, the two of us tackling one challenge after another, merging our skills, battling sleepiness like superheroes bent on saving the world.

Danillo appears at some point deep in the night.

"All right! A boat! And the dream team's at work on it. Morning departure?"

"You betcha," I reply. "Everything okay in the cabin?"

"Everyone's snoozing but me. Gabriel crashed after baking us a cake. I brought you some slices."

The moist chocolate melts in my mouth; I ignore the boat grease on my hands as I shovel in the rest.

"Awesome," Arturo says with his mouth full.

"Later, guys," Danillo says as he heads back up the stairs, and it's back to work, the quiet disturbed only by the loud *whooo* of an owl.

"Owls are sneaky," Arturo quotes me. "They fly silent at night but no can see everything. And eat more-small owls."

I pause and study him under the hanging bulbs.

"Like guards at camp," he continues. "I think Captain not know camp so bad. Was tricked. Maybe will understand."

Arturo's still loyal to the captain, I reflect uneasily. Still thinks the captain will return for him. Maybe the captain still owes him a bunch of money he needs. Well, at least he didn't alert the guards or stop us from escaping. In fact, his idea for trapping the men was brilliant.

For the next few hours, we chat about boat mechanics, the kinds of boats we'd like to own one day, tree planting, Guatemala City, ocean storms, and birds. He's pleased when I correct his English. It makes the time fly by; it keeps us awake. He's my friend — the first I've really had since Gregor abandoned me. I'd forgotten how chill it is to fix boats and yak alongside a buddy. I'd forgotten on purpose. And it occurs to me, not for the first time, that Arturo needs a friend, too.

It takes seven hours for the batteries to recharge. By then, we've drained the water from the fuel filter, found a replacement fuel filter cartridge, repaired the throttle cable, and checked and added oil. As the first rays of dawn hit, we collapse into the tug's torn vinyl seats with our feet up.

"Why you come back to camp?" Arturo asks me after a few moments. "Why not escape by self?"

"Pequeño."

He nods.

"I came back even though my brother told me not to," I say sleepily, not really meaning to let that slip.

"*Qué?* Brother in Ontario?"

"Sometimes I imagine talking with him."

"Pequeño say this brother in gang."

I frown. Evidently there are no secrets in this group. "Yeah, he went to jail."

"Goody-goody Owen has bad-boy brother?" He says it almost gleefully.

I give him a sour smile. "You don't know anything. I was in the gang, too."

"You?" His eyebrows shoot up.

"It started out him and me hot-wiring boats just for kicks. To go on joyrides together. It was fun."

"Uh-huh."

"Sometimes Gregor had friends who joined us. Then they started offering him money to hot-wire boats they wanted to steal. Not from our marina, but from around the harbour."

"He do it and get caught?"

"Yes, and put in juvie jail."

"What is juvie jail?"

"Youth detention centre. So the gang came to me. Dared *me* to hot-wire boats."

Arturo waits for me to continue.

"I like dares. And they treated me like I was a friend. I didn't have many friends of my own 'cause I always hung out with Gregor. And now he was gone."

"They pay you good money?"

"Yes. And I never got caught. Then Gregor gets released and comes home. Tells me off. Orders me to stay away from them."

"But you no listen?"

"No. One night I hot-wire them a boat and we go out cruising. But a storm comes up. The boat's too small for the conditions. We're getting whipped around bad. I'm scared. And then another boat comes speeding at us."

"Pirates?"

"No — Gregor. He's as angry as the wind and thunder. He comes close, holding a life ring with a rope attached, and shouts at me to jump. I can't decide what to do, but I've never seen him so upset or determined looking. And he's taking a big risk, trying to come alongside us in the big chop.

"The gang threatens to ram him if he doesn't leave us alone. He gets up close and tosses the life ring. I leap into the water and grab it."

"What then?" Arturo prods, because I've gone silent.

"The boys aim the stolen boat at Gregor's boat and throttle straight at him, even though I'm screaming at them to stop. He's standing in the bow trying to pull me in. He loses his balance and falls into the water, and the gang's boat hits his head."

Arturo is staring at me, wide-eyed.

"I get to him, put the life ring around him, and tow him to the swim platform while the gang speeds away. I pull him on board somehow. He's messed up, but breathing."

I have to take some deep breaths myself, I'm so choked up.

"Uh-huh?"

"I call the Coast Guard. They arrive fast."

"And?" he breaks the silence.

"That's why I want to join the Coast Guard. They rescue people."

"Your brother return to juvie jail?"

I don't reply.

"You go to jail?"

I shake my head.

"Your parents know?"

I shake my head again.

"So he protect you, gang get away, and gang no says you with them."

I stay silent.

To my surprise, Arturo moves closer and rests a comforting hand on my shoulder. "Say truth."

I find myself shaking. I've never told anyone. But it comes out — slowly, then faster.

"The Coast Guard ... got there too late." Arturo lets the silence stretch as if knowing there's more. "My parents and the Coast Guard ... they still think it was just Gregor and me there. The two of us overboard in the storm. No gang around."

Again, comfort in silence. Then, "Sorry, Owen. I understand."

"Understand?" It comes out like a croak. "How can you understand?"

Next thing I know, he tells me a wild story about his "family": how he got street boys work shining shoes, protected them, and one night hid them in a dumpster. But they were found. Every one of them. My stomach turns over. And I recognize the guilt and anguish in his voice; it steams off him just like it's steaming off me.

"I'm sorry," is all I can say when he finishes. I rest my hand on his shoulder. He lets it stay there a minute.

"If anyone learns you lie to Coast Guard, you in trouble. No can join Coast Guard." He sits back and crosses his arms, like he has solved some big mystery.

"What makes you think that?" I ask, voice shaky. Should I have told him anything?

"Should turn yourself in," he declares quietly and unexpectedly, his face turning serious.

"What?"

"Is big weight on you. Gang is guilty of trying to murder. No fair to brother they go free."

"Like people smuggling is on you?" I reply quietly. "I'll turn myself in when you do."

"Okay."

I'm trying to figure out what that means when the owl's *whooo* makes us jump. We study one another, joined by some invisible new bond.

"Why you pretend talk to your brother?" Arturo asks.

"Don't you have anyone you miss a lot, that you still need advice from?"

He takes a deep breath. "Captain," comes out in such a low voice that I hope I've heard him wrong.

"You think the captain cares about you?" I try to say it kindly. "He only cares about money. He's a vulture, a greedy vulture. Remember what I told you about vultures? If they're disturbed while eating, they vomit to make themselves light enough to fly away. That's what the captain will do to you or the boys one day. Upchuck you into the sea when he needs to flee."

"I know."

Before I can contemplate this surprise response, Danillo's voice jars us as he appears in the boathouse doorway.

"What's happening?" He's staring at us curiously. What has he overheard? "Thought you two were fixing up a getaway vehicle."

Arturo stands up quickly and brushes dust off his clothes. "We fix boat. Is ready. How is Pequeño?"

"His fever has broken and the twins are sounding a little better," Danillo says. "Come up for the spaghetti breakfast Gabriel has fixed. Then you two can get some sleep below decks on this thing while I drive."

• • •

ARTURO

Gabriel is stirring the pot of spaghetti on the stove. I glimpse Danillo stepping into the cabin's bathroom, opening the medicine cabinet, and sliding a container of pills into his jeans pocket. For Pequeño in case he worsens, I assume.

In the kitchen, Danillo helps scoop the steaming spaghetti onto plates and serves Owen and me first. Imagine that: a client serving me! I allow a smile before I start slurping it down.

"You guys deserve it," he says.

"Sweet!" Owen says as Danillo smiles and stoops like a waiter with a towel over one arm to serve him a mug of coffee. "You even found creamer and sugar."

I'm amused as he serves me coffee next.

It doesn't take long to polish off the spaghetti and clear the table.

"Let's get out of here before those guards get free and their boss traces us to here," Owen reminds everyone. "Don't know about you, but I've had enough of pushing trees into the ground."

"Got — that — right," Sergio says between coughs.

I step over to place my hand on Pequeño's forehead. He is still weak and sleepy, but less hot to the touch. I breathe a sigh of relief, then turn toward Gabriel, who is showing more colour in his face after a good sleep and some food. He is up to his elbows in suds as he washes the breakfast dishes.

"Is my job," I insist, moving into the kitchen. I cannot believe Gabriel has done all the cooking and dishwashing, though it is true I was busy repairing the boat. I am far more used to being put down and ordered around by the schoolboys, and being invisible when they do not need anything.

"Not anymore," Danillo says. "You're one of us now."

My breath catches and I dare to meet Danillo's eyes, which are friendly and reassuring. Am I really one of them? Could I be? Or will they turn on me when it is convenient?

My chest goes prickly and tight, then feels like it is being pulled in two directions. I have heard of people smugglers getting amnesty. They dress like their clients so if the group is caught, they blend in. If none of their customers identifies them, officers assume they, too, are smuggled would-be immigrants. Then they get treated the same as their customers. Freed, if they are lucky. Given a chance to live and work in another country, build a new life. But it is a big risk. Too dependent on the goodwill of people I cannot trust.

I breathe out slowly and mentally whack any temptation to fully trust them. Instead, I picture the cool bundle of cash Captain is holding for me.

Soon the cabin is shipshape. Owen places the note to its owners in full view and the boys file down the steps with their sacks. Pequeño no longer needs to be carried, though he is still weak, pale, and quiet. I glance back at the white van. Someone will come for it eventually. Stanton. I shiver and hurry after the group.

CHAPTER FOURTEEN

OWEN

As dawn lightens the sky, I feel beyond exhausted. More than a week of back-breaking labour on starvation rations, a gnarly escape, a long drive, and a full night of boat repair. No wonder my body aches for sleep! Add to that a plateful of spaghetti and hot coffee, followed by the nerve-wracking job of starting up *Homeward Bound*.

All eyes are on me as I position the jumper cables on the starter solenoid. *Er-er-er-rrrum!* We cheer like someone has scored in overtime as the engine turns over and the boat comes alive. It revs up, then calmly revs down as Arturo brings the throttle back to idle. "I can navigate for a while," he offers. Never have I been so drowsy as the guys generously award me the bed in *Homeward Bound*'s modest, musty stateroom.

Before I collapse, I dig out the map in the tug's chart table, point to the *X* that probably identifies this property, and mark where Powell River is. Then hand it to the guys. It's the nearest place for finding a doctor, contacting my parents, getting the authorities to start processing the boys, filing a report on the tree-planting camp using illegals, and reporting the captain's operation, I figure. Although I know I'll be held a while for questioning, I'm hoping that, with any luck, I'll be home and resting in a few days.

"Thanks, guys," I say, relieved that the boat is in good hands.

I sink into the soft embrace of the bed. Finally, I'm homeward bound and as happy as I am spent. There are ripples of guilt and anxiety at the thought of explaining things to my parents and the authorities, but it doesn't take long for exhaustion to vaporize those.

My thoughts drift like the clouds I can glimpse through the stateroom's Plexiglas port light: fluffy, floating, joining, and then separating like giant balls of soft dandelion fluff. Soon I'm up there with them, wafting and soaring, being drawn into a deeper dreamland than I've ever visited before.

• • •

Tap tap tap. Screech! Tap tap tap. I wake, startled and gradually aware of the dank smell of an old boat and sweaty sheets. The *tap tap* is familiar even if my brain is fuzzy. It's the noise of seagulls fighting over a scrap and the strut of their webbed feet as they waddle atop the port light over my head.

Port light? Seagulls? Where am I? On a boat, it seems.

I sit up, shake my foggy head, and resist the temptation to collapse back into the pillows. I'm in a stateroom and it's too small to be *Archimedes*. Of course! It's the tugboat we found at the cabin. I remember falling asleep as we left in the morning. But the port light above me indicates it's morning again. Have I really slept for twenty-four hours? My limbs feel heavy and my brain like cotton wool, almost as if I've been drugged.

Tap tap tap. Screech! Tap tap tap. I peer upward. A seagull cocks its head and peers back. Chunks of bread form strange silhouettes on the Plexiglas. That's what the birds are pecking at.

I listen intently. No engine, no boys, nothing but lapping waves. So we're anchored. Maybe at Powell River? Scrambling out of bed, I charge through the lower level and note that the boys' duffle bags remain scattered. Up to the deck. *Screeech!* The seagulls lift off and flap away.

I peer at the brightening sky and notice a reddish tone. Red sky at night, sailor's delight. Red sky at morning, sailor's warning. Before I can process that thought, Danillo greets me from the deck of *Archimedes* a few feet away: "Look, he's awake!"

Huh? Sebastian is lying on his stomach with a camera aimed at otters in the bay. Danillo is playing chess with Sergio, and Gabriel appears in an oversized apron and oven mitts, holding a pan of slightly burned cookies.

"I tossed some bread over there to see if I could get some bird photos," Sebastian explains. "Was hoping for something more interesting than seagulls. Sorry if they woke you up."

I look around the isolated bay the two boats are in. There's no landmark to indicate where in the Strait we are. Then I lean down and, with one angry sweep of my arm, send the bread slices flying into the drink.

"Where are we and what's going on?" I demand. I glimpse Pequeño dozing on *Archimedes*'s salon sofa and Arturo lifting the black metal frying pan from its rack and dropping in refried beans, cheese, and bananas.

"Well, well, look who's finally up," says the captain, strolling out on *Archimedes*'s deck. "Welcome back to the world."

"Checkmate!" Danillo calls out, exhilarated, as Sergio's shoulders sag.

"Arturo, rustle up a late lunch for Sleeping Beauty here. What would you like, Owen? Two eggs over easy on toast, bacon, raspberry jam, orange juice, and coffee with cream and sugar, as usual? And Gabriel has been baking. I need to fatten you all up after that terrible experience, yes?"

I look from Danillo to the twins to Gabriel. No hint of traitor's guilt or unease. They look perfectly contented. Maybe I slept through some kind of time warp? I should have stayed awake, helped direct where we were going!

The captain pulls on the rope that hitches *Homeward Bound* to *Archimedes* until the two boats' rails are touching. Then he holds out his muscled, tattooed forearm to help me across.

Do I have a choice? I take the leap.

"Sit down, sit down, boy," the captain says as the schoolboys resume their activities. I sit and turn to look at Arturo, but he's still got his back turned to me as he bends over the stove.

"So, you all put in five days of tree planting, just two days short of what was needed. I guess I understand your desire to quit early, given the conditions — assuming you aren't all exaggerating." He chuckles. "And Arturo did the right thing saving Pequeño, although there will be hell to pay with my friend who arranged everything, especially over the lock-up trick."

He coughs; Arturo's body twitches.

"In any case, each of the boys has phoned his parents, who've paid up the equivalent for those missed days of work. Therefore I'll release everyone tomorrow. In Comox, where you, Owen, can catch your ferry."

"But what about *Homeward Bound*?" I demand, dumbfounded.

The captain laughs. "Well, we're not towing it to Comox, so I guess it'll stay anchored here till someone finds it."

"How — how did the boys find you?" I ask, trying hard to get my head around everything and trying to stay alert despite a dark, sinking feeling.

"By phone, of course," the captain replies. "As soon as your cute little tugboat passed near a point with service, Danillo called me, and I directed him here."

"Called you? You mean from a public phone on a dock?"

The captain laughs again. "No! From Arturo's cellphone, which my first mate tells me didn't work from the labour camp."

"He had a cellphone the entire time?" I can't help blurting out. My friend betrayed me while I slept? Maybe even drugged me to make me sleep?

"Yes. I believe you loaned it to him?" As the captain fishes a cellphone out of his pocket, I grab it from his hands. It's mine. It disappeared the night of the storm, the first time Arturo visited me. So he stole it and has had it all this time? Angrily, I start to punch in my parents' number, only to realize it's dead. I flip it over and tear off the back panel. The battery has been removed.

"Calm yourself, little stowaway. I confiscated the battery this morning, when Danillo turned it over to me. But it'll be easy enough to buy new batteries in Comox. Anyway, I have to get back to the bridge to plot our course. Eat heartily, boy, and the clients will keep an eye on you if you get bored."

That sounds like a threat. He slaps me lightly on my shoulders; my body tenses like an iron rod.

I stare at Arturo's back again; this time I see bloodstains that have leached through. Like he's had a fall. Or a lashing. He turns to serve me my breakfast and backs away quickly. But not before I see purple bruises around both eyes. His punishment, or the first phase of it, for being part of our early departure from the tree-planting camp and the lock-up escapade, I figure, regardless of what the captain just said.

I look at my plate. Sure enough, two eggs over easy on toast, bacon, raspberry jam, and coffee with cream and sugar. The smell wafts up to my nostrils. My still-shrunken stomach growls noisily. But I stand, carry it over to the sink, and dump it all in, pouring the steaming coffee on top.

Arturo's jaw loosens a little.

"Could be poisoned for all I know," I say, and stride out to the deck.

"It wasn't me," Arturo hisses, but I ignore him.

"Game of chess?" I ask Danillo, trying to keep my voice calm and even.

"If you dare," he responds. The other boys drift back into the salon.

"Why?" I ask in a low voice as we position our pawns.

"Easy," he replies in barely a whisper. "If we had disappeared, he would have hurt our families."

My jaw goes slack. My heart pauses. Nothing like that had ever occurred to me.

"He knows where our families live in Guatemala City. A deal's a deal. Now it's all settled and good. I slipped some crushed-up sleeping pills from the cabin into your and Arturo's coffees, because I didn't trust the two of you to take us back."

I resist upending the chessboard in his face. Instead, I grit my teeth and play chess while contemplating matters well beyond the game in front of me.

• • •

ARTURO

I do my best to look calm, but I can hear my heart ticking like a time bomb. Beatings? I've had enough of them for a lifetime. Next time he raises those fists ... And good luck to Danillo if he dares to cross me again, either.

I push the stowaway's breakfast into the garbage, squirt dish soap forcefully into the sink, finish the dishes, and limp toward the bridge.

"Arturo," Gabriel calls out.

I swing around, way too tired to fill another order. Unlike Owen, I have not slept off all the drugs Danillo put into my coffee at the cabin. I forced my eyelids to stay open for more than an hour while piloting the tug, but eventually turned things over to Danillo and tumbled into bed. How was I supposed to know he would point *Homeward Bound* to *Archimedes*'s cove before my first snore?

"I saw you once back at the camp using that cellphone. Stole it from your bag while you were asleep on *Homeward Bound*," Danillo explained when we arrived. "Lucky for me it still worked. Sorry about doping you, but wasn't sure whose side you'd be on about turning *Homeward Bound* back toward where Captain was waiting."

I lean over the stern railing and spit just to see how far it will fly.

"Arturo, play Battleship with me?" comes Gabriel's voice now.

The smile comes to my swollen lips slowly. On the surface, everything looks the same. But nothing's the same. Not the way the boys are treating me. And not me, ever since the *Homeward Bound* all-nighter.

"Later, Gabriel," I say. "Good cookies, by the way." Well, edible this time.

"Arturo?"

"Yes, Pequeño?" I move to the sofa and brush the boy's hair out of his eyes, pleased to see colour returning to the cheeks. Pequeño smiles. "I got to talk to my mom and dad."

"I heard you."

"I can make cookies, too, you know. I'll make you some later."

"Sounds good, kid. Can I put a movie on for you?"

"Nope, I can do it myself."

This is the only boatload of clients I'll ever miss.

"Need some more ointment on your wounds?" Danillo asks, holding the first-aid kit he brought to my bed soon after the Captain was finished with me.

"I'm okay," I say, a lump in my throat. "Thanks anyway."

I heave a big sigh and haul myself up the companionway to the bridge. "May I sleep now, Captain?" I ask, certain my body will collapse soon if I do not get serious rest.

"Soon, Arturo," comes the deep-voiced reply, laced with slightly less venom than when the group of us arrived hours earlier. "First we meet in my stateroom for a brief conference."

The word makes me shiver.

"Okay." I hesitate, wanting to ask for my pay, but decide to wait until Comox. I turn and make my way down the companionway.

Captain will buck up after the clients are gone, I tell myself. It'll be just the two of us down the coast again, heading home. Nicer weather will hit; heading back south is always easier than battling northwesterlies on the way up. If I work hard all the way, Captain will give me that raise. I deserve a gazillion dollars.

It was foolish of me to imagine escaping from Captain. Leaving the tree-planting camp was wrong, and I deserved to be punished, but I did it for Pequeño. No regrets.

CHAPTER FIFTEEN

OWEN

The flag on *Archimedes*'s bow flaps in a wind gust that draws me out of my worry over where I just moved my king. I shiver and study the sky.

"The wind has just changed direction and the temperature's dropping," I say to Danillo.

"So?"

"And the sky has a weird feeling to it, don't you think?"

"You're just trying to distract me 'cause I'm winning. But yeah, the clouds are a little pea-green over there," he says.

"Means a storm is coming," I say.

"Oh, you're an expert weather forecaster, are you? Well I just took your queen, so boo hoo."

"Congratulations." My voice is a little icy, since I haven't forgiven him for drugging Arturo and me and hijacking the tug back to the captain. But something tells me I have to play along for now until I can determine if the captain really will deliver me to Comox, or I see an opportunity to escape.

I smile distractedly. "I'm going to ask the captain when we're leaving."

"Suit yourself," he says as I rise and wander up to the bridge.

"Captain, can I help with anything?" I ask.

"You stay off the bridge. That's an order!" he snaps.

Whoa, grumpy today or what? "Okay. May I ask when we're leaving?"

"Soon."

"Good. 'Cause I think a storm's coming."

I turn and start down the companionway when he addresses me in an entirely different tone. "Actually, gather the boys, Owen. We need to transfer their gear from *Homeward Bound* to *Archimedes*, and I wouldn't mind a look at the tug while we're over there."

"Sure." I get the boys' attention and we make our way along the deck.

"The tug's older and less flashy than *Archimedes*, but strong as a bull," I tell the captain.

Danillo and Arturo, the first mate avoiding my eyes, draw *Homeward Bound* and *Archimedes* together by pulling on the ropes like a tug-of-war. One by one, the boys clamber over the rails. Danillo even does a show-off cartwheel without managing to fall into the water. The twins, still coughing but less than before, coordinate pulling Pequeño over like he's a ragdoll. Gabriel leaps and laughs. Finally, the captain, Arturo, and I climb soberly from the yacht to the tug. As Arturo releases the ropes, the boats move apart like untethered horses toss-ing their manes, wary of one another.

Arturo heads for the pilothouse and slumps into the captain's seat. His jaw set, one fist clenched. His eyes have a haunted look as he rests his other hand on the tug's tool box and stares into the Strait. Like he's not with us, not one of us.

The guy has hardly slept in the last thirty-six hours, I calculate, if you add together our last tree-planting day, the escape, the drive, the all-night tug-repair session, the navigation of *Homeward Bound* till he slept briefly, and the time he has spent being drugged, beaten up, and ordered around since.

"Hope you get some sleep soon," I say.

"Get out of here," he grumbles as he slips something from his fist into the small drawer under the chart table and slams it shut.

The captain is opening cupboards, examining the pilothouse engine gauges and controls, and fiddling with the radio.

"Boys!" he calls cheerily, and we gather around him. "How did you like the ride on this?"

"Okay, but not as comfy as *Archimedes*," Pequeño says.

"Smells bad, like rot," Gabriel offers.

"Arturo and Owen worked all night on it," Danillo states while doing chin-ups on the companionway hatch.

"Yeah?" the captain responds, turning his gaze to me. "I don't see any keys. How did you get it started?"

"We put jumper cables on the starter solenoid and it turned over, first time," I boast.

"Well done," he says. "Show me."

Within minutes, I have the jumper cables positioned again. *Er-er-er-rrrum!* Arturo, still sitting in the pilot-house, adjusts the idle. We jump as he suddenly blows his whistle hard, three times.

"Boat approaching," he calls down in a worried voice.

Like a well-programmed squadron, we take one look at the captain's panicked face and look around for somewhere to hide.

"Quick, down there," the captain suggests, pointing to the engine compartment. We tumble down into it, knowing it's the only refuge *Homeward Bound* offers.

I find myself squashed up in the dark between Danillo and Pequeño, just feet from the diesel stench of the engine. Another robbery or the Coast Guard? I wonder. We hear the captain's heavy footfalls; he's sprinting to the pilothouse.

There are shouts, I hear the captain bellow, "Back off!" and then two reports of a firearm. My heart pounds louder than the engine beside us and sweat snakes down my neck. Vibrations of footfalls in every direction confuse us. Who's aboard and who's going where? What if they find us?

From beside us, *Homeward Bound*'s engine suddenly revs up. We place our hands over our ears; the boys closest to the whirling prop shaft lean into the rest of us. The fumes pour like toxic waste into our lungs. Our throats tighten to gasping. Then there's a creak and some pitching as the tug moves forward. Slowly, then faster. Soon, it seems to be hurtling at breakneck speed. Well, breakneck speed for a tug. Why? Who's at the controls?

Pequeño is shaking beside me; I'm straining my ears toward the hatch. No voices, just the stomp of boots running around the boat. Maybe stealing things?

Smash! I start at the sound of glass breaking, as if dozens of drinking glasses are falling from a shelf. Then an ear-splitting pounding of steel on steel that seems to reverberate through our very nerves. I'm so clenched up that I almost forget to breathe. What is going on? It's like our vessel is being taken apart at the seams in an iron scrapyard.

Just as I'm thinking of bursting out and grabbing something for a weapon, the thunder of footfalls funnels immediately over our heads and to the rear. Dust filters through the hatch cracks in their wake. Now a thud and a splash — something or someone heavy hitting the water. More shouts, an outboard motor starting and then roaring away.

Definitely not the Coast Guard. I wipe sweat from where it's trickling down my forehead.

We wait for the captain or Arturo to blow the all-clear whistle. We wait and wait, ears peeled. An agony of moments passes. Nothing. No voices, no sounds but the din of the engine and the crash of bow waves.

Finally I rise and pull on the latch of the hatch door. It doesn't click open. Danillo jumps up to help me. We push and all but assault it. The twins rise and strain like they're lifting barbells at a competition. It won't budge.

"Someone has locked us in," Sebastian rules.

• • •

ARTURO

Captain and I are the last to climb from the yacht to the tug. We're pretending it's all about the clients transferring their gear and letting Captain have a look at *Homeward Bound*.

I have my orders, and Captain has a gun. Captain and I are about to pull off Operation Destruction.

"They'll make it to shore or get rescued by the Coast Guard," Captain assured me during our whispered conference on *Archimedes*. "They'll be free in no time at all." Then he laughed. "We'll be long gone, the real homeward-bounders."

I head for *Homeward Bound*'s pilothouse and plop down into the captain's seat. The very place where Owen and I had our all-night repair and reveal session. Must not think of that now. I clench my fist around something Captain doesn't know I have. It's my own personal Operation Defiance.

"You remembered your whistle?" Captain checks.

"Yes." It feels heavy hanging around my neck. I raise my fingers to touch it and get an electric shock. I gaze into the grey, stormy Strait, waiting and fighting to stay awake.

"Hope you get some sleep soon," Owen says as he passes by.

"Get out of here," I reply, pressing my lips together to keep any other words from escaping. Then I slip what's in my hand into the small drawer under the chart table and slam it shut. He startles at the slam. He'll remember.

He has to remember later. I'd slip what I have directly into his hand, but then the scene won't play out like it's supposed to, and Captain has his Glock at the ready.

"I don't see any keys in the ignition," Captain is saying on cue to Owen. "How did you get this boat started?"

"We put jumper cables on the starter solenoid and it turned over, first time."

"Well done," he says. "Show me."

Within minutes, the tug jumps to life. *Er-er-er-rrrum!* An echo of my heartbeat.

Now!

I lift the whistle to my lips. It slips out of my mouth and dangles. I lift it again. I'm under orders and Captain has a gun. And my pay.

Screech! "Boat approaching!" I call down in a voice I hope sounds worried.

I am supposed to be first mate, not an actor in a badly written play.

"Quick, down there," Captain delivers his line, pointing to the engine compartment.

They fall for it, as we knew they would. I don't hear the click of the lock, but I wince for the schoolboys anyway.

Captain sprints to the pilothouse, shouts to the invisible pirates, and shoots his Glock off twice. Then we stomp around to make it sound like there are more than just the two of us.

Back in the captain's seat, I ramp up the tug's speed like the pro I am, then reach into the tool box. The crowbar feels as cold as ice. It rises and comes down hard, following Captain's orders against my will.

Smash! Bang! With Captain beside me wielding a sledgehammer in one hand, a giant wrench in the other, the tug doesn't stand a chance. We're a two-man demolition crew. He lays into the boat with a fury that sets my nerves on edge. Though I fail to mimic the fever of his assault, I work alongside him, fuelled by my own fireball of anger.

The throttle is the first to go. Soon the entire dashboard all but collapses under our attack. The window shatters and controls break and spin through the air like body parts.

Within moments, all the mechanics that Owen and I lovingly coaxed back to working order are in pieces. Then, without a backward glance, we thunder through the tug to the dinghy, our escape vehicle. With a loud splash, it hits the water. I tumble into the bow. Captain jumps into the stern, pulls the cord of the outboard motor, and we roar away through blackening swells that rise and crash.

We're headed back to *Archimedes*, of course. My body shivers and shakes as I hang on in the dinghy's bow. Spray soaks and chills us as we race away from the driverless tug lumbering in the Strait. I look back once to see it lurching through the waves, no hand on the controls, a half dozen boys locked in its belly. We've abandoned what is now a moving ghost ship. A death boat. A Dumpster full of innocent souls — friends? — betrayed. By *me*.

I breathe, breathe, breathe to calm myself down.

A small cut in my hand from the smashing drips blood into the saltwater sloshing at my feet. But I feel like gore is smeared all over my body.

I am not convinced someone will rescue them in time, now that we have finished the job. My brain is spinning, my stomach is lurching, my body is so gripped with guilt that it is threatening to shut down.

I look up to see two eagles soaring confidently overhead. Half a dozen ravens flap haphazardly away in the other direction.

Captain is in the stern with a smile of boyish excitement. "They paid to come to Canada, they're in Canada, and we're rich," he shouts. "Better yet, we've just eliminated our chances of getting in trouble during the dropping-off process."

"Uh-huh," I say dully.

"I'll pay you when we get back aboard *Archimedes*, Arturo. Damned good job you did. You're the best. Time for a raise, yes?" He leans forward to slap me on the shoulder. I wince like his touch has electrocuted me. I cannot stand to look at him.

I've been with Captain for three years. I've learned lots of things on this job and put up with its dark side: the beatings and the feeling sometimes that I'm a captive slave. I've always reasoned my way through the bad times, blamed myself or excused Captain or weighed my chances of doing any better if I left.

But he has never done anything cruel to the clients, let alone ditched them. Maybe he suspected I was getting in cahoots with Owen? That I was going to jump ship? That I was pissed about having to plant trees? Maybe Danillo overheard some of Owen's and my conversation the night we repaired *Homeward Bound*, and reported something?

No. As far as Captain knows, I totally co-operated on the destruction of the tug's controls. To him, I'm still a fully loyal first mate.

My stomach goes sour; the world turns white as I puke over the dinghy's side. I retch everything I have in me into the speeding grey water. But everything I have in me is not enough. As my head hangs over the gun- wale, I sense that the water wants to rise and swallow the rest of my useless self.

"A seasick sailor!" Captain jabs, shaking his head. "Well, you'll feel better for that."

I may not deserve this cool job, but I will do absolutely any- thing it takes to keep it. Did I believe that once? No, not anything, as it turns out. Not this. But what could I do?

You don't have to be his lackey.

I'm not. You'll see.

He's cruel. You're not. He doesn't deserve you. You deserve better.

I do. And it's not too late. I'm sorry, I know it looks like I failed, guys. To break the chain. But all is not as it seems.

"When opportunity presents itself, take it," Captain reminds me, beaming a proud grin. "Cheer up, boy. You can sleep while I pilot tonight. You've earned that."

"*Gracias, Capitán.*" Sleep, yes. I've earned it. On this we can agree.

CHAPTER SIXTEEN

OWEN

The smell of diesel, rot, and desperation in the air is overpowering.

"We need a crowbar or something," I rule, looking about the cramped engine room with the headlamp I always carry on me.

"How about ripping out that pipe?" Sergio asks, pointing to a steel pipe.

"No!" I shout. "I mean no, that's the exhaust," I say more calmly. "It'll fill the compartment with engine exhaust and we will die."

Gabriel is feeling around the bulkhead in front of us for anything else that might work, and casting his eyes around the floor.

"Over there, under the prop shaft?" he suggests, his head frighteningly close to the spinning shaft coupler. "Hey, I see an iron rod. Can't ... reach ..."

"I can get it!" Pequeño's high voice declares.

"No way you're squeezing under —" I begin, but Pequeño has wriggled too far away from me to yank him back.

"Flatten yourself to the floor and back out if —"

"Touching it!"

"Careful," the older boys chorus with me in tight voices.

"Got it!" the kid shouts.

The shaft spins and throws off a threatening *thump thump thump* that hurts my ears as it continues to send 150 horses down to the propeller.

Pequeño worms backward inch by inch. I bite my tongue when he screams; the shaft has snagged a tuft of his hair. Then he's clear, turns around, and hands his prize to me.

"Nope," I say, shaking my head. "This is a job for the twins." I pass the iron tool to them.

Smash! Smash! Dust and splinters come raining down as the young giants apply the iron rod to the hatch. We close our eyes and raise our arms to cover our heads as the twins go at the cover like medieval warriors applying a battering ram to castle doors.

Smash! Crunch.

"Yes!" they shout.

A second of quiet, then Sebastian pokes a hand through the hole they've created. *Click!* The hatch is unlocked. As he lifts the hatch cover, we erupt out, me holding Pequeño up until the boy finds his footing.

Four pairs of feet scurry up the companionway after Pequeño and me. We stop short in front of the wrecked helm.

"Captain? Arturo?" Pequeño calls out uselessly, leaning into the wind blowing through the missing windshield.

"He locked us in and then sabotaged our boat!" Danillo cries out. "Bastard! He has his money and he's trying to kill us so we can't identify him. I'll try an SOS on the radio." A second later, his panicked voice: "No go. Cable to the mic is cut."

I elbow my way into the space, braced against the wind's force and the cold rain, and stare open-mouthed at the destruction. It's like something hit by a grenade: shards of glass everywhere, a torn windowsill, smashed fuel gauges all caved in, a gaping hole where the tachometer and voltmeter should be. The bent oil-pressure gauge has one needle sticking straight up at the ceiling.

The knot meter is gone too, but I guess we're doing around 8.5 knots. My hands move automatically to the wheel. Try as I might to turn it, it won't budge. It's like the wheel and shaft are welded into their current position. Worse, the throttle controls are lying on the control-room floor. I sink into the captain's seat with my head in my hands.

Sorry, owners. I forgot to include mention of this kind of damage in the note on your cabin table.

Something stings my cheek. I look up and realize that the rain is morphing into hail. Black, anvil-shaped clouds are on the horizon and the wave action is beginning to bounce us about. We are a death machine hurtling toward whatever rocks are fated to destroy us, if we don't capsize first during what is becoming a major storm.

"Owen?" It's Danillo, with the rest of the Guatemalan pack half cowering behind him. Everyone is studying me, waiting for signals, commands, assurances that they're not on a high-speed death cruise. "How do we stop it?"

"We don't," I say, bracing myself as *Homeward Bound* rises on a foaming crest and plunges into a deep grey trough.

"Huh?" the chess master questions.

"If we stop, the waves will devour us. We're like a bicycle — better off moving in these conditions."

"But can we steer it?" Sebastian asks, touching the useless wheel and frowning.

"Or slow down before we hit shore?" Gabriel asks in a tremulous voice.

"Maybe," I say, lost in thought. "Everyone get lifejackets on. I'm going to hunt for whatever fire extinguishers are on board. Gabriel, get something to cover this broken window. Danillo, you're on watch for deadheads, rocks, and land. Pequeño, grab every cushion, mattress, and pillow on board and pile them on the stateroom bed."

"Why?" he asks, eyes large.

"They'll be our air bags if we crash."

"What about Sergio and me?" Sebastian asks, standing beside his brother.

"I need your muscles, you two. I need every ounce of strength you've got."

"For?"

"Turning the boat. First, we're going to use the carbide hacksaw in the tool box to cut off the steering cable. Then I need you to go below and fetch that heavy bar you used to break out of the engine room. The one with a square knob at the top. It's actually the boat's emergency tiller, and you are going to be our helmsmen."

"Huh?"

"This way —" I point to the left side of boat "— is port. The other side is starboard. Once we get the emergency tiller set up, you'll position yourselves on either side of the tiller in the engine room, and I'll yell down to you to move it one way or the other. Sergio, your name is now 'Port Sergio' and you'll sit on the left side. When I call 'port' you'll push the tiller away from you. Sebastian, your name is now 'Starboard Sebastian' and you'll sit on the right side. When I call out 'starboard,' you'll push it away from you. When Sergio pulls, Sebastian pushes, and when Sebastian pulls, Sergio pushes."

"We can do that," they say with nervous coughs.

"Good," I say as confidently as I can. It's our only chance. I find myself wishing Arturo was on board to consult with. That's when I remember the sulky-looking first mate dropping something into the chart table drawer.

He wanted me to see him do that. My shaking fingers gravitate toward the drawer. They linger just short of it. Then they pull on the knob. My cellphone battery lies just inside.

"Yes!" I whisper. "Arturo's on our side!"

Sprinting to the head, I pull out my cellphone, insert the battery, and punch in numbers with shaking fingers.

"Dad?" I say, my breath catching. "Dad, Mom! It's me!"

• • •

ARTURO

I get my pay. A nice wad of bills. I should be happy. But I am miserable and scary tired.

"Sleep, Arturo," Captain says in a kindly voice. "Sleep till we're home if you like!"

"*Gracias.*" I move down the companionway like a sleepwalker, clutching the handrails as the yacht tosses drunkenly.

"Sure you are okay in these conditions?" I call up to Captain. More importantly, what will this storm do to *Homeward Bound*? And did Captain really have to lock the boys in besides destroying the controls? They'll find a way out, won't they? At least the phone battery I snuck into the drawer will allow them to call for help.

"*Archimedes* is built for worse than this," Captain asserts.

And it is riding higher because you lightened your ballast. The same way vultures do when they want to make themselves light enough to fly away.

"But even so," Captain continues, "I'm taking us to the nearest bay to wait it out."

"Good call," I dare to say.

I collapse into bed. Despite my desire to escape, my throbbing head and raw stomach, the sweat soaking my sheets, and a hot ache in my cut hand, I plunge into an uneasy sleep. In my dreams, I am chased by tree-planting guards, Coast Guard officers, angry clients, ghost ships, Guatemala City police, and vomiting vultures.

CHAPTER SEVENTEEN

OWEN

Balls of hail hit *Homeward Bound* from all sides like a barrage of bullets. The gale-force wind from the southeast is something like forty knots, yet it doesn't slow our determined tug for a moment. It may not know where it's going, but it's hell-bent on getting there.

"How much fuel do we have?" Danillo asks me.

"Started with half tanks and this model uses about eight gallons an hour, so we've probably burned up only half of what we have."

"Sounds good. That's enough to get us somewhere safe, right? And you've figured out how to stop this thing when it's time?"

"I have."

"Hungry?" Gabriel asks as he enters the pilothouse. We turn to the welcome sight and smell of two steaming plates of baked beans.

"Don't know about Danillo, but I'm starving," I reply. "You're the man, Gabriel."

Danillo and I scoop spoonfuls into our mouths.

"Look, they're not burned! Way to go," Danillo teases.

Gabriel smirks.

"Thanks for getting the plastic in place on the window, too," I say. It offers a flapping, blurred view of the frothing sea, but that's way better than a gale in my face.

"You're welcome. The twins say they're ready."

"Okay. Port!" I shout. I can actually hear Port Sergio grunting and groaning like an animal as he pushes the emergency tiller. Slowly, *Homeward Bound* begins to turn left.

"Starboard," I shout, testing Starboard Sebastian. *Homeward Bound* nudges the other direction.

"Hurray! We can steer!" Danillo enthuses. "Now we can keep it in the middle of the channel and off rocks."

"Exactly! Are you willing to stand watch while I check on things below?"

"Of course."

With one eye on the Strait along which we're hurtling, I move about, collecting up the tug's life ring buoys. Soon they're weighing down my right arm like a jangle of giant bracelets.

Each is twenty inches in diameter, weighs three pounds, and offers a minimum buoyancy of 16.5 pounds, I recite to myself. Made of solid closed-cell foam, UV resistant, with straps and reflective tape. We have the same kind on our dock, ninety dollars apiece. Each has a rope, which I busy myself attaching to the bow rail. They're all Coast Guard regulation life rings, of course. And I can throw them thirty feet.

Next I walk down the companionway to see how Pequeño's doing with the air bag project in the forward stateroom. It's all set up, and my young friend is sprawled amongst the cushions, sleeping again. He is doing okay for someone still recovering from a lousy sickness.

It's the first time I've been in the tug's stateroom in full daylight, and I'm puzzled to spot a pillowcase hanging on the rear partition wall, or bulkhead.

It's the pillowcase I slept on — and it was definitely not there when I left the tug earlier this morning. More curiously, it's hung like it's trying to hide something. I snap the fabric off and catch my breath. I'm staring at a swing mount — like a little gate tucked into the wall, visible from the bridge just above us only when swung out into the companionway. OMG! It holds a recently installed Garmin GPS chart plotter!

No way! How did Arturo and I miss it when we were fixing the tug? In our defence, it was dark, we were tired, and we were focused only on the engine room and bridge. We never went forward to where it was fully stowed out of the way. Gingerly, I unlatch the arm and swing it aft to view it, then remember Danillo and tuck it back where it was.

"What's up?" Danillo asks as I appear beside him.

I stand over the captain's seat. "Take a break, Danillo. I'm good."

"Okay." He looks curious but doesn't ask why I'm flushed with excitement as he goes below.

During their bash-up party, Arturo must have spotted the folded-away Garmin and covered it up in hopes the captain wouldn't see and surely destroy it.

I look up at the radio mounted on the ceiling of the wheelhouse. Its microphone cable has been cut, but all we need is for it to receive. I cross my fingers and turn it on. "At least it has power," I whisper. "But what about GPS?" My heart leaps as the navigation computer boots up and displays the words *position acquired*.

I swing the arm into the pilothouse and select AIS on the Garmin; that's the Automatic Identification System that uses a vessel's GPS, marine radio, and transceiver to identify other AIS-equipped vessels in the area.

Archimedes has AIS! Captain never imagined we could turn this tug around, let alone identify exactly where he is now and hunt him down.

"Port! Starboard!" I command in turn for the next few minutes. Slowly, thrillingly, *Homeward Bound*'s heading responds. "Great work, Sergio and Sebastian," I call out, truly appreciating their hard labour, especially now that the waves are growing violent. "You two are heroes!"

I imagine their body odour filling the engine compartment and cusses sounding between their pushing and pulling.

"Just a little more," I notify them, watching the little image of our vessel on the chart plotter plod along the channel.

Danillo steps onto the bridge. His face is as stormy as the Strait. "You've done a full U-turn," he observes. "Why would you want to turn completely around when we were headed toward Comox?"

"You'll see in approximately ninety minutes," I calculate. "Trust me, Danillo. You owe me that after drugging me."

He looks at his watch, throws me a glare, and disappears without noticing the arm.

• • •

Over the next hour and a half, the wind blasts us like something intent on blowing out our makeshift windshield, while the waves toss us until the boys are barfing over the side. Worse, rogue waves threaten to swamp us once or twice. My teeth are so gritted they hurt, but with my tillermen's help, we remain upright and ploughing doggedly forward.

"Feels like an out-of-control roller coaster ride," a pale-faced Gabriel says when he brings me coffee at one point.

"It's nasty out there, but don't underestimate this tough old tug," I respond.

• • •

It's less than ninety minutes before I call out, "Port! Port! A little more port, Sergio! Okay, stop! Steady as she goes."

Danillo reappears. "So explain yourself," he orders, lifting a corner of the would-be window to gaze out. "Why did you turn us around?"

I hand him the binoculars.

He peers through them and straightens up suddenly. "Look, there's land ahead! We're turning into a bay!

And there's a boat anchored there! Coast Guard?" he asks me eagerly.

Funny how the school bunch has been afraid of the Coast Guard till today, but now they're ready to embrace any kind of rescue.

"No," I reply, checking my watch and eyeing the tiny image of *Archimedes* on the chart plotter, which is just another piece of equipment to most of these guys.

Gabriel snatches the binoculars from Danillo. "Land ahoy, everyone! And there's a boat we're pointed straight at!"

The others spill into the pilothouse. "A big boat," Pequeño elaborates when he manages to wrestle the binoculars away from Gabriel. "Yacht."

"More than forty feet long," Gabriel guesses.

"No way. Is that —" Pequeño starts.

"*Archimedes*?" Danillo finishes.

"The one and only," I declare.

"*Archimedes*?" The twins echo in horror from their stations.

"Starboard! Starboard!" Sergio calls out to Sebastian. "We don't want to go anywhere near them!"

"Oh, yes we do," I call out calmly.

A knuckle presses into my Adam's apple and my head slams against wood panelling as Danillo grabs the front of my sweatshirt, pulls me up out of the captain's seat, and pushes me up against the pilothouse wall. "How'd you track them down, Owen? And why? Captain's got a gun, you know. He had a second one hidden that he has been carrying around since the pirates stole his other one. What are you trying to do, you maniac?"

"I'm not trying to do anything," I lie, slipping from his hold and reseating myself. "But it sure seems like there's a wounded tug wanting to take revenge on a bully yacht. And since the controls aren't functioning, it's out of our hands."

"Oh no, it's not!" Danillo says in a fierce voice.

"Hey!" Sebastian shouts. "Stop fighting and tell us how to turn this around before it's too late!"

"Owen," Gabriel pleads, "how do we stop? We can't go hitting *Archimedes*. It's way bigger."

"It's not the size of the bird that matters," I instruct them. "It's the size of the talons. Or the flock."

"He has lost it," Sergio rules, having abandoned his station to grab the binoculars and see *Archimedes* for himself. "Danillo, take over the controls."

"*What* controls?" Danillo screams back.

I leap up. "It's okay, guys. We're not going to smash into *Archimedes*. I'm going to spray the fire extinguishers into *Homeward Bound*'s engine compartment when we're about a hundred feet away from the yacht. That will kill the engine by starving it of oxygen. The tug will slow from eight to two knots in about thirty seconds. At most, we'll give *Archimedes* a nudge. Just enough to scare them."

"You mean scare them into shooting at us?" Danillo barks. "What's this really all about, Owen? Talk to us if you haven't lost your mind!"

"Okay. We've come back to give Arturo a chance to jump ship."

"Arturo? You're totally nuts!" Gabriel declares.

Now they're all screaming at me. Danillo raises his fists in front of my face; his voice goes shrill. "Captain has a gun, I said. Didn't you hear me? And Arturo will do anything Captain says. He just helped Captain smash up the controls, in case you missed that! They got their money, they're on the run, and both of them want us dead. Give Arturo a chance to jump ship? No way!"

They're right. Not worth it, bro, Gregor weighs in. *Should never have turned around this sorry excuse for a boat. You're dealing with nasty elements. Didn't I teach you anything?*

"You taught me well, and it's time to make my own decisions, Gregor."

"Who the hell's Gregor?" Sebastian wants to know. "Now Owen's talking to himself, everyone!"

"The Coast Guard is on the way, cutter and helicopter," I inform them. "Courtesy of Arturo, who does *not* want us to die. He left us my cellphone battery, and my guess is he stopped the captain from destroying the Garmin chart plotter."

"*What* Garmin chart plotter?" Danillo asks in a stunned voice. His face reddens as I point to the fully functioning little screen on the foldaway arm.

"I reckon Arturo needs off *Archimedes* before the Coast Guard shows up and the captain turns the gun on him," I continue, "and I'm going to give him that opportunity."

The boys stare at me, open-mouthed.

"Arturo left your phone battery?" Danillo repeats.

"So we could call for rescue," I confirm. "And I believe he saved the chart plotter from the captain's sledgehammer."

There's a moment of silence.

"I believe you," Danillo says. "I believe Arturo would do that."

"Maybe Arturo didn't want to smash up the tug, but Captain would've shot him if he hadn't," Gabriel reasons.

"I'm glad you agree. But I couldn't take the chance that you wouldn't," I say, staring at Danillo until he looks away. "Especially since —"

"We deceived you. We didn't give you reason to trust us," he concedes with a shrug. "Sorry." The others nod silently.

"I waited till the phone had reception for a moment," I continue, "and called in our position and situation to the Coast Guard. Besides talking to my parents."

"I never heard you," Gabriel challenges.

"From the head while you guys were distracted."

The boys lift a corner of the tug's plastic windshield to scan the dark, tumultuous ocean for our saviours. None visible yet.

I study the outline of *Archimedes*, now clearly identifiable without binoculars, then stare at my watch while doing some math in my head. We're about 150 yards out. *Archimedes* is moored lying head to wind, and *Homeward Bound* is tracking straight at the centre of it. They've spotted us. I can see the captain on deck, open mouthed and staring into his binoculars.

"It's time for Sergio and Sebastian to get out of the engine room," I tell everyone soberly. "Pretty soon I'll release the fire extinguishers to kill the engine."

"You don't need us to steer after the engine stops?" Sergio asks.

"You'll suffocate if you're in there when I spray," I inform them, "and we'll reach *Archimedes* a minute after that. So, right now, everyone needs to get down to the stateroom's bouncy castle feature. Surround yourself with the cushions, ready for impact. Keep your heads down and away from the portholes."

They move fast, with no argument. When I figure we're nearing a hundred feet from the yacht, I kneel beside the engine compartment hatch, holding two five-pound fire extinguishers. With great care, I insert their nozzles down the hole the twins made with the pipe.

Three, two, one — *spurt!* The bottles do a heavy sigh each while emitting their noxious fumes below. The second they're spent, I drop them and sprint to the bow. It takes an agonizing ten seconds for the tug to lurch in response. Then there's the sputtering and clattering of an unhappy engine and the subtle slowing of a tug-turned-missile.

• • •

ARTURO

The cold splashes of saltwater bring me to.

"*Mierda!*" I swear.

Captain is standing over me with a dripping bucket. "Wake up, Arturo. *Homeward Bound*'s in sight. I thought you pointed it west before we disabled her."

"I did!" I leap up, trying to hide a smile. He is coming back for me!

Captain pushes me to the floor and rests a boot on my neck. "What did you do? They should have hit something, sprung some leaks, and sunk by now!"

"But you said —"

"They're liabilities, Arturo," he says as he pulls his belt off his trousers. "Don't you get that? It's not like other trips. Too many things have gone wrong. We can't have them talking. And no one would have blamed their wreck on us. But somehow they've boomeranged."

"Boomeranged, Captain?" An English expression I do not know. While an electrical charge I do know is ramping up inside me.

"They've gotten enough control of that bitch-tug to turn it completely around. I need you to lift anchor so we can get underway, now!" The belt slices through the air and lays its sting on wounds not healed from the last whipping. Pain sears through me. "I'm thinking you sabotaged our sabotage."

"I didn't, Captain!" At least, not in the way Captain thinks. The truth is, I can guess how Owen managed to spin the tug around. I am both impressed and happy about the turn of events.

We scramble up to the bridge.

"See anyone aboard?" I ask Captain, who has the binoculars pressed to his eyes.

"No one."

"Maybe it really is a ghost ship?" I say in Spanish. "Maybe the boys bailed before it boomeranged?" Cool new word, that.

"Impossible. Don't be stupid." But a note of fear has crept into his voice.

"There are missiles that can lock in on a target and —"

"It's a rustbucket tug, not a war machine! Doesn't even have AIS or steering! But that pig has its snout pointed right at us." His hands grip *Archimedes*'s wheel so tightly that his knuckles turn white.

Keep pretending you're onside till you can get away. "We can outrun them, Captain. *Archimedes* is a way better boat."

"Of course we can! So stop talking and move!" he bellows as he starts the engine. "Pull up the anchor! It's your fault that thing has come back from the dead!"

I run out of the pilothouse onto the bow. I am not expecting the force of the wind to almost fling me off my feet. Hail slaps my face like flying glass crystals, and even though we are at anchor, we are being bucked about by waves barrelling into shore.

The storm is way worse now than when I fell asleep. Good thing Captain agreed to wait it out. As for *Homeward*

Bound, it is amazing none of the swells out there has swamped her. Owen must be piloting.

The tug's older and less flashy than Archimedes, *but strong as a bull.* Owen's words echo in my ears.

A bull like Ruffian, charging toward us at this very moment.

I draw my hoodie around my face to protect me from the hail and glance up at the black sky. Captain won't move the boat forward till I operate the windlass to lift the anchor. I'll just take my time. I listen to the *clink, clink* of the windlass as I draw out the usual three-minute procedure. From the corner of my eye, I see Captain pacing back and forth on the bridge and the tug bearing down.

Did Owen get through to the Coast Guard? Does the Coast Guard fly in weather like this? And surely Owen is intending to rescue me, not ram *Archimedes*?

The story of Owen's brother rescuing him comes rushing back to me.

He's holding a life ring with a rope attached, and shouts at me to jump. I've never seen him so upset or determined. And he's taking a big risk, trying to come alongside us in the big chop.

It's like all the current in Guatemala City's power stations is diverting into my body. I abandon the windlass and run aft while shouting, "Captain, I need to reset the windlass hydraulic-pump circuit breaker!"

"Fast!" Captain's panicked voice barks.

I race down the companionway, grab my tin of money from the broom closet, buckle on a lifejacket, and sprint to the swim platform, ready to leap.

"Oh no you don't," Captain says, panting as much as me as he steps down from the fly bridge. His elbow closes around my neck and the cold metal of his Glock presses into my cheek.

CHAPTER EIGHTEEN

OWEN

If I were driving a car in a Hollywood car-chase scene, I'd perform what's called a handbrake turn. Forward full speed, brake, and spin on a dime with the tires smoking. It's called doing a donut. Or a quarter of a donut, really.

In ideal ocean conditions — which we're definitely not experiencing now — I could put *Homeward Bound*'s engine in neutral, then reverse and manoeuvre the helm with just the right timing to park parallel to the yacht. That would impress the moustache right off the captain.

But given what I've got to work with, the best I can hope for is to nudge *Archimedes* before it ships anchor and heads out of the bay. What I don't want to do is plunge so deeply into the yacht that I "hole" it and it sinks, especially since Arturo could be locked in the dog cage. But we have to get close enough for Arturo to do his team switcheroo if he can. Which I'm counting on him wanting to do.

Like you?

"Yes, Gregor, like when you came for me. You gave me a second chance."

Not the same. Riskier.

"I'm not listening to you anymore."

I've noticed. Why?

"Because I always wanted to be like you, but I'm not you, and you can be a bad influence on me. It was your gang that adopted me back in Ontario."

It was me who told you to get out after you made the bad decision to get in. And me who saved your ass that stormy night.

"Okay, okay, have it your way. And I tried to save you. I really did."

The hail turns to rain, which streams down my face.

I know, little bro. His voice is gentler. *You're right. It's time to be your own person now. A better person than I was.*

"Gregor, I can do this because you taught me well."

Then I'll butt out. But remember my last words: Stay clean, and never tell Mom and Dad you were part of the gang. We were out there boating together, no stolen boat in sight.

"And you died from hitting your head on our boat when you fell in the water. No other boat was involved. They still believe that, you know. Mom, Dad, and the Coast Guard. The guys never talked, of course."

I know.

"But Mom, Dad, and the Coast Guard were suspicious. Why else would Mom and Dad have moved me to the other side of the country?"

I understand. I miss you, Owen. We're both sorry the Coast Guard didn't get there on time. But you've kept our secret and stayed clean since. I'm proud of you.

Proud of me keeping a secret that feels like a three-hundred-pound barbell on my shoulders? But I don't say that.

Ahead of us, *Archimedes* swings on its anchor line.

Less than a hundred feet between the two vessels. *Homeward Bound* is tracking fairly straight, but it's going to be close. I run to the bow and convert myself to a ship's figurehead as I lean forward over the bow railing, a tethered life ring in hand.

There's no one in *Archimedes*'s pilothouse, as far as I can tell. That's strange. And no one visible on deck or peeping out the portholes. My attention focuses on movement in the stern. What I see there turns my blood cold: Arturo on the swim platform, and the captain leaping down and pointing a gun at him.

At the same time, I hear a roll of thunder louder than any that has yet sounded today. Instead of roaring and growing quieter, however, it keeps booming, accompanied by a *whack, whack* of lightning.

Lightning or helicopter blades? Through the darkness of the clouds at the head of the bay, I hear it before I see its searchlights. My heart soars.

"Jump, Arturo!" I scream.

We're closing in. Seventy-five feet: the distance that Olympic discus champs can throw. But I'm not one of them.

I lift the life ring to my chest. My heartbeat is drumming so loudly in my ears, I can barely register the clatter of the helicopter approaching. *Homeward Bound* is now sixty feet from *Archimedes*. Fifty feet.

I see the captain and Arturo look my way. We're close enough now to see the whites of each other's eyes.

My hand squeezes the life ring like I'm intent on denting it. But my mind is measuring, measuring. Like a warplane bomber pilot who must drop his load with precision timing.

The helicopter dips down, all seven thousand pounds of it, an angry bird descending in a cacophony of whipping steel blades.

We're forty feet from the yacht. Estimated moment of impact seconds away.

The captain shifts his Glock to aim at me; shivers run down my spine. Then he raises it toward the unarmed Coast Guard Bell 212 Twin Huey.

My wrist flicks back and I let her rip, the ring toss throw of my life. *Wham!* The captain doesn't see it coming, but Arturo does. It knocks the gun out of the older man's hand, making him loosen his grip on the first mate. As the Glock slides across the deck, Arturo's formerly white boating shoes connect with it to send it full speed into the drink. A split second later, Arturo scoops up the life ring and leaps.

Pull, pull, pull. I'm staggering down the starboard side of *Homeward Bound*, my hands wrapped to the point of cramping around the rope that runs between the bow, where it's tied, to the life ring Arturo grips in the water. Using the railing as leverage, I run my hands down the rope to drag him toward the stern, Gregor adding his own muscle and ensuring that I don't get pulled overboard. He knows what could happen if we don't get Arturo to safety.

Pull, pull, pull. Together, Gregor and I haul Arturo up to the swim platform. With a final, superhuman yank, we land him. Then all three of us cling to each other and to the nearest railings.

As the rain lashes, the helicopter hovers, the boys downstairs brace, and the captain dives into *Archimedes*'s salon, the two boats slam.

With an otherworldly screech, *Homeward Bound*'s bow rides up and over *Archimedes*'s beam, taking out the stanchions — the upright posts supporting the railings — on the yacht's port side. The tug rises halfway over the gunnels, shudders, then slowly slides back, pulling the stainless-steel lifelines with it. Next comes a high-pitched grating sound as the yacht's torn railings snag on *Homeward Bound*'s bow-mounted anchor.

And then, as gently as it pounced, the tug separates and rafts up alongside, directed by the tangled, buckled lines holding the two boats together.

Only one person disappears overboard, never to speak to me again: my brother. His departure leaves a hole in my chest the size of the Pacific Ocean. But I know in my wrung-out heart that it is time. Time to set him free. Time to accept he's gone. Time to live life without him.

• • •

ARTURO

Seconds tick by as I lie face down on the tug's aft platform, soaked and shaking. One hand maintains a death grip on the life ring; the other clings to the wire cable beside me. I am waiting for the tug to buck again — and this time maybe slide me back into the water. Is the crash over yet?

"Arturo, Arturo, are you okay?" It is Owen, his face pale, his hands locked around my wrists.

"Yes," I say, erupting into shivers as the electricity in my veins drains away. I allow him to pull me into the tug's salon and wrap a blanket around me. "I-I boomerang to you. Wh-where's Captain?"

"We collided and he —"

"A cutter! A Coast Guard cutter!" Shouts come from deeper inside the tug. I turn my head to see Danillo, Gabriel, Pequeño, and the twins stampede up the companionway and point out to the Strait. "A Coast Guard ship! Coming for us!"

"I knew they'd come!" Owen says with a victor's smile as I tighten into a ball and reach for my whistle — then relax and drop it.

"Thanks for coming back —" I start, but they are not listening to me. One by one, Owen leading, they sprint to the railings and jump over onto *Archimedes*. Even Pequeño, though he moves more slowly. Why not wait on board the tug till the Coast Guard arrives — they're too impulsive, these boys. Always have been.

"Careful!" I shout, struggling up and lumbering to the deck. I can see Captain's boots sticking out of *Archimedes*'s salon on the aft deck, unmoving. I stand and steady myself on the tug's railing, clutching my blanket around me.

The boys surround the still body of the big man.

"Careful!" I shout again, not trusting my boss to be truly knocked out. I climb over the railing myself and place one hand on my pocketknife. But by the time I reach the group, Danillo has opened the engine room hatch, dropped down, and flipped the dog cage over so that its gate is at the top. Above him, the twins each grip the man's underarms and lower him, with help from Owen, Gabriel, and Pequeño, like they're slipping a king salmon into the hold.

"*Mierda!*" Captain growls as he comes to en route. Pequeño flips the gate shut and Danillo snaps the lock on.

Captain raises his head with difficulty and glowers at me.

"Sorry, Captain," I explain, "but we keep a tight ship."

CHAPTER NINETEEN

OWEN

The sound of a pistol shot rivets our attention.

"Are they going to shoot us?" Pequeño asks, posed to dive into his old hiding place on *Archimedes*.

"It's not a gun," I explain. "It's a warning shot across our bow because we're not up there answering Channel 16."

"What's Channel 16?" Gabriel asks.

"I'll explain later. We need to file out on deck, slowly." I look at Arturo. "They won't hurt you," I try to reassure him. "They're not even armed."

"Canadian Coast Guard orders you to stand down for boarding," booms a stern but familiar voice through a bullhorn.

I beam, but the smile fades fast.

"Everyone out on deck, hands in the air," the voice continues.

Danillo leads, followed by the twins, Gabriel, and Pequeño. Head bowed, I fall into place behind Arturo.

"Okay, alert crew to board to starboard," Officer

Olsen directs his team. "Steady as she goes. Now hard to port and come alongside."

My pulse is pounding in my ears, mosh-pit hard. It's all too familiar, and yet this time I'm on the wrong side of what is decidedly *not* a simulated exercise.

"Is this all of you? Anyone else on board?" the bull-horn demands.

"Yes, Officer Olsen, the coyote — the captain — is restrained below deck," I say.

There's a pause.

"Owen?" Officer Olsen shouts, lowering his bull-horn. "Owen Steward!"

I nod at him, my face hot under the gaze of the boys. "By the way, we got robbed by the grey-bearded pirate and his gang. His beard is fake."

"You don't say."

Soon the Coast Guard team has swarmed the boat, handcuffed the captain, and checked every nook and cranny. Every nook and cranny means not a boy would have been left unfound. Pretty clued in, these Coast Guard dudes and dudettes.

We're still standing in line on the deck, shivering in the wind-driven icy rain.

Officer Olsen walks up and down, staring at us. I can't meet his eyes.

"Captain," he addresses his prize prisoner, "which of the boys are your paying customers, and which are your helpers?"

The captain says nothing, just glares at the Coast Guard intruders.

"Boys, who in this lineup worked with your captain? We know he didn't operate this vessel on his own all the way up from Guatemala."

No one steps forward. No one says a thing.

"Owen! Can you identify who was in cahoots with the captain?" Officer Olsen demands. "We can't have criminals trying to sneak in as refugee claimants." He lifts a pair of handcuffs to emphasize his point. "Then you can go rest up on our cutter," he adds.

My eyes are glued to the deck. My lips are zipped. Arturo has gone stiff beside me. There's no way I'm betraying him, no matter how much trouble that causes me.

"I am Captain's helper," Arturo says, stepping forward.

"Don't cuff him!" I shout as Officer Olsen leans forward to grab Arturo's arms. "He turned against the captain! He saved us! We wouldn't be alive if it weren't for him!"

Officer Olsen hesitates.

"It's true," Danillo says.

"Arturo deserves to stay in Canada," Gabriel insists.

Officer Olsen takes his time looking from one to the other of us. He narrows his eyes as we move to encircle Arturo.

"He's our friend," Sebastian shouts as Sergio nods.

I catch the hint of a smile pass over the first mate's face. He slowly removes a pocket knife from his jeans and hands it over to Officer Olsen.

The captain makes a rude noise and spits.

Finally, my Coast Guard friend stuffs the cuffs back in his pocket. "Okay, crew, take them below decks on our vessel and get them blankets and water. "Owen," he adds gently, putting his hands on my shoulders and steering me away, "you've obviously been through an ordeal. I need to radio Search and Rescue and you need to contact your parents —"

"Did that already, same time as I called the Coast Guard."

"Oh. Okay, good. We'll question you when you're ready, but you need rest, and from the looks of you, some food. You need to get out of those wet clothes and away from here. Follow me to our galley and I'll fix you some coffee —"

"Is his favourite drink," Arturo speaks up, smiling at me. "He like cream and sugar. And if I stay in Canada," he continues, directing his words at me, "I make you gazillion eggs over easy. And help you with boat repairs."

"We can catch fish off your dock, right? I'll grill them," Gabriel speaks up.

"I want to take that water taxi to school," Pequeño says.

"You and I will dominate the school chess team," Danillo teases.

"And Sergio and I will star on the wrestling team," Sebastian announces.

My chest loosens a little; a half smile replaces the threat of tears. "That's for sure," I tell everyone.

Turning away from a puzzled-looking Officer Olsen, I say, "So much for being a loner on a boring island."

"Boring?" Arturo objects. "Paradise, *idiota*."

My smile broadens as Officer Olsen leads me away. "Thanks for letting me join your school cruise. It has been a gazillion kinds of interesting, and we'll stay in touch."

CHAPTER TWENTY

OWEN

They're sitting on our dock, shoes trailing in the June water, looking forty-nine kinds of anxious, when the Coast Guard cutter rounds the point into Steward Bay. I'm at the helm of the sixty-five-foot vessel. Yes, I'm captain and top dog, complete with the navy-and-white Coast Guard cap and double-breasted jacket with gold buttons and stripes on the cuffs. Never mind that Officer Olsen's uniform hangs on me a little, or that his hands hover over mine on the wheel.

"Hi, Mom and Dad," I call through the bullhorn.

They leap up, smiling, the flood of relief and pride as easy to read as a calm sea on a blue-sky day. They also look like they've aged several years over the past two weeks.

"Thanks, Officer Olsen," I say, and swallow hard before shaking his hand, shedding his uniform, and sauntering down the gangplank. Maybe I'm too old for it, but I throw myself right into my parents' waiting arms.

"I'm sorry, sorry, sorry," I breathe.

"You're home," Mom whispers, hugging me tight as tears roll down her face.

"That's all that matters," Dad adds.

We wave to the crew as they back the cutter out of the marina like it's a simple ketch. No scrapes or hesitation. Damn, they're good. But it's okay that I may never be one of them now.

"I've got coffee on," Mom says. "Sandwiches waiting upstairs. Some reporters are coming around later, like we mentioned on the phone."

We've talked several times since that first call from *Homeward Bound*, of course. But I'm not having any of the celebrity business yet.

"Mom, Dad, there's something I have to tell you. It's about Gregor and me."

The joy drains from their faces, but I have to do this now, before I lose my nerve.

"Can't it wait, dear? You've only just arrived."

"It can wait one hundred and twenty steps," I allow. "I'll tell you over lunch."

"Okay," Dad says warily.

I nearly slip on a mossy step. And the loose one creaks. I smile. Lots of chores for a marina maintenance slave while he's grounded forever. Along with catching up on schoolwork.

"I would have left you a note," I say, "but when I snuck aboard, I never imagined —"

"Of course you didn't," Dad says. "I mean, what were the chances? I remember the time you and Gregor stowed away —"

Oops. Mom's tears are flowing full force now. And we've arrived at the top of the steps.

We file in and sit down at the kitchen table. Smells good in here, like fresh-baked muffins. I help myself to coffee and place a sandwich on my plate.

"There's something Gregor made me promise never to tell you," I begin, "and that's a promise I can't keep anymore."

Mom's hand moves toward Dad's, who covers it with his.

"After Gregor went to jail, I got pulled into his gang."

"We suspected that," Dad says. "It's why we moved."

"I was with the gang the night of the storm. We stole boats."

There's a loud sigh. They study the kitchen table. I'm too choked up to carry on for a minute.

"He came out in another boat to rescue me and to get me away from them. He'd been trying to talk me into quitting the gang for a while."

Dad nods and squeezes Mom's hand.

"Gregor stood in the bow with a life buoy on a rope, shouting at me to jump. He tossed it in. But when I jumped —"

Mom is trembling.

"Go on, son," Dad says, his voice tense.

"He fell in just as the guys deliberately tried to ram his boat. Their boat hit his head."

Mom is weeping, Dad is holding her, and I cup my face in my hands. I wait a few minutes to continue.

"I got the life ring around him, hauled him onto the boat, and called the Coast Guard as the gang took off in their stolen boat. The boat *we* had just stolen," I clarify. "Coast Guard didn't get there before Gregor ... His last words were to never tell you."

Dad is nodding slowly, his eyes wet. Mom has buried her head in his chest.

"So you never reported these guys," Dad says. "And you told us it was just Gregor and you — an accident."

"Yes." My voice comes out like a squeak. "He didn't want me to get a police record. Otherwise I could never join the Coast Guard."

"But you're telling us now," Mom says, voice shaky.

"And I told Officer Olsen. Yesterday," I say soberly, meeting her eyes.

She reaches out to hold my hand. "You've done the right thing, Owen. We'll be able to press charges against the gang. You know we always suspected, right?"

"But it's my fault, Mom. My fault he died." My chest shudders and heaves like an earthquake that has been waiting to release pressure for a century.

"That's not true, son, and you know it," Dad says.

"We forgive you, Owen."

I lower my head and breathe deeply. "I don't deserve it, but thank you."

"Now tell us everything about your kidnapping — I mean, your stowaway adventure."

. . .

An hour later, taking a breather before reporters descend on us, I pedal my bike around the island. Past the bird blind, the bakery, and the general store. I wave at islanders who grin and shake their heads at me. I bike all the way to the bull field.

"Hey, Ruffian." I stop and lean on my handlebars. "Know what? I used to think you were the most dangerous thing on this island. Guess what? You've been demoted."

He chomps on grass and eyes me like he hasn't missed me a bit. He doesn't even raise his head when an unkindness of ravens gets into a flap with an eagle overhead.

"But here's the good news. Our island isn't boring after all. Turns out it's chill. It's awesome big time. It's paradise. And you and I are lucky enough to live here."

SAVING LIVES AT SEA

Many deaths by drowning (including those of young children) result from vessels being overcrowded with refugees attempting to reach safe shores. Unfortunately, organizations capable of rescuing them, like the Coast Guard, have limited resources. To help prevent tragedies, the Migrant Offshore Aid Station (MOAS), based in Malta, operates boats to offer food, water, and medicine to migrants in need. They also escort at-risk vessels to shore so their occupants can apply for asylum. At the time of this writing, MOAS has saved more than twelve thousand lives. Pam Withers encourages readers to fundraise for this organization. A percentage of profits from this novel will be donated to MOAS. For information, visit www.moas.eu.

ACKNOWLEDGEMENTS

Section 6.1c, Moorage Law Covenants: You must provide without compensation temporary accommodation to any vessel that is disabled or that seeks shelter in weather conditions that would render it unseaworthy.

This paragraph appeared in the real estate contract involving our cabin's dock. Reading it was all it took to launch this story.

Above all, I'm indebted to editor extraordinaire Janice Weaver. Also to copy editor Catharine Chen, proofreader Kathryn Bassett, assistant project editor Jenny McWha, and all the team at Dundurn Press. Very special thanks to my patient mariner consultants, Mark Evans, Allen Slade, and Dennise Dombroski. And to Joseph and Laurie Payne, who allowed me to tour their Hans Christian Independence 45 while it moored in Horton Bay on Mayne Island (the inspiration for Horton Island) in British Columbia. For a plate of fresh-baked cookies and an autographed book that I delivered by kayak, they even allowed me to photograph their engine room, closets, and other potential hiding places.

Special thanks to my tree-planting son, Jeremy, and to Charlotte Gill's beautifully written *Eating Dirt: Deep Forests, Big Timber, and Life with the Tree-Planting Tribe*. Sober acknowledgement of the Congolese workers treated like slaves at a tree-planting camp in Golden, British Columbia, in 2010 (B.C. Human Rights Tribunal case against Khaira Enterprises).

Appreciation to Malcolm Scruggs, my outgoing teen editor, and Vansh Bali, my incoming teen editor (I fire 'em when they turn eighteen ☺). Vansh truly went above and beyond on this one! Warm thanks to Lynn Bennett, my agent; Maggie de Vries, author and writing workshop leader; Steve, my husband; Shannon Young and Silvana Bevilacqua, valued friends; and the Mayne Island Writers Group, especially Leanne Dyck.

Recommended further reading and viewing: Wolfgang Bauer's gripping *Crossing the Sea: With Syrians on the Exodus to Europe*; *How I Became the Mr. Big of People Smuggling* by Martin Chambers; *The Jaguar's Children* by John Vaillant; and *The Devil's Highway* by Luis Alberto Urrea. Also, the movie *Frozen River*.